Zedekiah S. Barstow

Remember the Days of Old

Zedekiah S. Barstow

Remember the Days of Old

ISBN/EAN: 9783337264079

Printed in Europe, USA, Canada, Australia, Japan

Cover: Foto ©Andreas Hilbeck / pixelio.de

More available books at **www.hansebooks.com**

"REMEMBER THE DAYS OF OLD."

A

Semi-Centennial Discourse

PREACHED IN THE

FIRST CONGREGATIONAL CHURCH,

KEENE, NEW HAMPSHIRE,

JULY 1, 1868,

BY THE

REV. Z. S. BARSTOW, D.D.,

AT THE CLOSE OF HIS

FIFTY YEARS' PASTORATE.

PUBLISHED BY HIS CHILDREN

NEW YORK:
THOMAS WHITTAKER, PUBLISHER AND BOOKSELLER,
No. 2 BIBLE HOUSE.
1873.

" Remember the days of old; consider the years of many gener-ations ; ask thy father, and he will show thee ; thy elders, and they will tell thee." DEUT. XXXII. 7TH.

THIS is part of the song of Moses, which he uttered in the hearing of all Israel just before he ascended to the top of Pisgah, to behold the goodly land, and to die.

And I avail myself of these words, as a fit introduc-tion to what I would say, on this fiftieth anniversary of my ministry in this place. I invite you to " remember the days of old ; " to " consider " the hundred and thirty-four years that have passed, since the first movement for the settlement of this town.

The Proprietors' Book gives the following account of the beginning of things in Keene, then called the Upper Ashuelot:

Whereas the committee that have laid out the Home Lotts in the towns westward on Ashuelot River and Poquaig,* have notified all persons that are desirous to take up Lots on the terms and con-ditions this Court † has directed, to meet at Concord (Mass.) on Wednesday, the 26th instant ; and it being necessary after these Lots are drawn, that the grantees be assembled, and come into proper methods for the settlement of their said Lotts, etc., that after sixty persons for each township shall have drawn Lots, and given Bond, and paid their five pounds according to the order of this Court, July, 1732, that they forthwith assemble at Concord, and then and there chuse Moderator, Proprietor's Clerk, and agree upon Ruls and methods for the fulfilment of the respective grants, and to

---

* Athol.   † The General Court of Massachusetts.

make any further Divisions, and for calling other meetings for the uture, and any other matters or things for the speedy settlement of said towns..

Sent up for concurrence,
J. QUINCY, *Speaker.*
Council, June 19th, 1734.
Read and concurred,
J. WILLARD, *Sec'y.*
21st, consented to,
J. BELCHER, [*Gov.*]

A true copy Examined pr. SIMEON FROST, *Deputy Sec'y.*
A true copy Examined p. SAMUEL HAYWOOD, *Proprietors' Clerk.*

In pursuance of the above, on the 26th day of June, 1734, the General Court's Committee met at the house of Mr. Jonathan Bell, Inn-holder in Concord, Mass., in order to admit proprietors into the Upper Township, on Ashuelot River. The names of "S^d Committee are as followeth," viz:

WILLIAM DUDLEY, ESQ.,
EBENEZER BARREL, ESQ.,
DANIEL EPPS, ESQ.,
EDWARD GODDARD, ESQ.,
JOHN CHANDLER, ESQ.,
MR. SAMUEL CHANDLER,
MR. JOHN HODSON,
MR. ISRAEL WILLIAMS.

On the day above said, the said Honble Committee received as proprietors of the Upper Township on Ashuelot River, the persons hereafter named. Said grantees received their lots by draught, in order of the numbers affixed hereafter to their names respectively. Each grantee paid five pounds money to the said committee upon admittance, except the Minister and the Ministry, and School Lots: *

* Thus it appears that the proprietors paid three hundred pounds for these premises.

1. CAPT. SAMUEL SADEY,
2. JEREMIAH HALL,
3. SAMUEL HAYWOOD,
4. JOHN WITT,
5. JOSEPH WRIGHT,
6. JOSEPH FLOOD,
7. SOLOMON KEES,
8. JONATHAN MORTON,
9. THOMAS WEEKS,
10. ISAAC POWER,
11. WILLIAM HOATON,
12. EBENEZER ALLEN,
13. MINISTER LOT,
14. DANIEL HAWS,
15. JOHN HAWKS,
16 PHILEMON CHANDLER,
17. ROBERT MOOR,
18. ISRAEL HOW,
19. WILLIAM WITT,
20. JONATHAN WHITNEY,
21. JOSEPH HILL,
22. WILLIAM PUFFER,
23. BARTHOLOMEW JONES,
24. JOSEPH PRIEST,
25. JONAS KEES,
26. WILLIAM SMEED,
27. JOSEPH HILL,
28. SCHOOL LOT,
29. MINISTRY LOT,
30. EDWARD HALL,
31. DAVID MOSS,

32. ISAAC HEATON,
33. DAVID CHANDLER,
34. BENJAMIN WHITNEY,
35. JOSEPH ALLEN,
36. NICHOLAS SPRAKE, JR.,
37. ABRAHAM MASTER,
38 NATHAN FAIRBANK,
39. NATHANIEL ROCKWOOD,
40. JOHN CORBETT,
41. JOHN GUILD,
42. JOSEPH ELLIS,
43. JOHN NIMS,
44. JONATHAN SOUTHWICK,
45. ROBERT GREY,
46. THOMAS ABBOTT,
47. JOSIAH FISHER,
48. JABEZ WARD,
49. ISAAC TOMBERLIN,
50. JONAS WILSON,
51. EBENEZER WITT,
52. AMOS FOSTER,
53 DAVID HARWOOD,
54. EDWARD TWIST,
55. JOHN BURGE,
56. EBENEZER MASON,
57. DANIEL HOAR,
58. ELISHA ROOT,
59. MARK FERREY,
60. JOSIAH FISHER,
61. ELIAS WITT,
62 SAMUEL WITT,

63. STEPHEN BLAKE.

At the time in question, it was supposed that the valley of the Ashuelot was in Massachusetts, and Governor Belcher, in 1732, recommended to the "Great and General Court, that care be taken to settle the ungranted lands."

At a general meeting of the Proprietors of the Upper Township on the Ashuelot River, on the 18th day of September, 1734, *held on said Township* by adjournment from the 27th day of June last past, "to make arrange-

ments for laying out roads, and building mills and procuring surveys of lands preparatory to settlement," it
was "propounded whether Messrs. Josiah Fisher of Ded-
ham, Samuel Witt of Marlboro, and John Hawks of
Deerfield, be a committee to survey the whole of the
entervail in said Township, etc. ; and that they have
liberty to Imploy a Surveyor, and Deacon Alexander, of
Northfield, to assist them. This was voted on the affirmative."

"Voted, that Messrs. Josiah Fisher, Samuel Witt, and
John Hawks, be a Committee to search and find the best
and most convenient way to travel from the Upper unto
the Lower Township." *

Among other votes then passed was this : " That this
meeting be adjourned until the last Wednesday of May
next, at 12 of the clock on said day, to be at the dwelling-house of Mr. Ephraim Jones, Inn-holder, in Concord," [Mass.]

Other meetings were held in Concord, Mass., from
time to time. But on the 30th September, 1736, a
meeting of the Proprietors was opened according to appointment, at the *house-lot* of Joseph Fisher; but was
immediately removed to *the house* of Nathan Blake.
This was probably the first house that was erected in
the township. No person had hitherto attempted to
winter in the place. Those who came in summer to
clear their lands, brought their provisions with them.
But in the summer of 1736, at least one house was built;
and Nathan Blake, Seth Heaton, and William Smeed,
made preparations to pass the winter in the wilderness.
Their house was at the lower end of Main Street. Mr.

---

* The Lower Township was afterwards named Swanzey.

Blake had a pair of oxen and a horse; and Mr. Heaton also, a horse. They had collected grass in the open spots, for the support of these beasts; and in the early part of the winter, they employed them in drawing logs to the saw-mill, which they had built on Beaver Brook. Mr. Blake's horse fell through the ice in Beaver Brook, and was drowned. In the beginning of February, their provisions were exhausted; and they sent Mr. Heaton to Northfield to procure supplies. But before he left Northfield, the snow began to fall; and when he arrived at Winchester, where there were a few families, it had become so deep, and covered with so sharp a crust, that he was told that "he might as well expect to die in Northfield, and rise again in Upper Ashuelot, as to ride thither on horseback." He nevertheless attempted it, but soon found it impossible to succeed. He then directed his course toward Wrentham. Messrs. Blake and Smeed soon gave their cattle free access to the hay, and on snow-shoes sought the abodes of civilization. Early in the Spring they returned, and found the oxen near the "Branch," below where Mr. Robinson resides. The oxen recognized their owner, and gave signs of pleasure, which drew tears from his eyes.*

When only one dwelling-house had been erected, the settlers were resolved to record God's name among them. It was on September 30th, 1736, that it was "voted that they would build a Meeting-House, at the Upper Township on Ashuelot so called, 40 feet long, 20 feet stud, and 30 and 5 feet wide; to underpinn, cover, and inclose the same, and lay down bords for the lower floor; and to set the same at the south end of the town street, at

* Vide Hale's Annals, p. 10.

the place appointed by the General Court's Committee; and that Messrs. Jeremiah Hall, Samuel Daniels, Joseph Richardson, Stephen Blake, and Josiah Fisher, be a Committee to build, or let the same; and to see that the S^d work be completely performed by the 26th day of June next." Thus you see that the first settlers of this place "could not come into the tabernacle of their house, nor go up into their bed, until they found out a place for the Lord, a habitation for the mighty God of Jacob." How different were they from some of their descendants and successors; who care not for the House of the Lord, nor for the sound of the church-going bell; nor for the exercises of prayer and praise!

After five years, (1741) that meeting-house, which was at the south end of Main Street, was removed to the middle of the street, south-east of where Gen. James Wilson's house now stands; the travel passing on the east side of it.

In the early part of the summer of 1737, and while few houses were yet built, it was "voted to assess the sum of 240 pounds on the Propriety, to support the preaching of the Gospel in said township, and other necessary charges arisen or arising in S^d Propriety."

It is not known how or when the Rev. Jacob Bacon, their first minister, came into the place. But it was during the same year above mentioned; for in October, 1737, it was voted "That the worthy Jacob Bacon draw the Lotts for the whole Propriety." This was at the second division of the meadow-land. In the course of the same year, he was appointed Proprietors' Clerk; and the first entries which he made in the Proprietors' Book, were in April, 1738. Mr. Bacon received a call to become their pastor, May 5th, 1738; gave an affirmative answer on the 5th of August following; and was ordained October 18th of the same year, when the church was organized: consisting of nineteen male members. It is evident from this, that the church was established before the wives of the settlers had come hither for a permanent residence in the place.

The following was the call presented to the Rev. Mr. Bacon by the Proprietors' Committee:

To MR. BACON,
WORTHY SIR:
We the subscribers being chosen a Committee by the Proprietors of the Upper Ashuelot, yᵉ fifth day of May Current to represent them in laying their proposals before yourselfe for your acceptance of yᵉ work of yᵉ ministry; which proposals are as followeth, (viz.:) First: the Proprietors by a unanimous vote choose yourselfe to be their minister; and in the second place, voted to give towards your settlement in Sᵈ Township yᵉ sum of one hundred and fifty pounds in Bills of Credit; and in the third place, they voted the sum of one hundred and thirty pounds of the Old Tenor, [£32 10 sterling] according to the present value of it * for your yearly salary, for ten years, and then add ten pounds to your yearly salary. These, Sir, are the proposals, which we desire yourselfe to take into your Consideration, in order to your acceptance; and humbly Desire your answer to us, (who have the whole affair committed to us by the Propriety) in a convenient time, that we may know what further is necessary to be done in this affair.

Sir, We are your humble servants,
JEREMIAH HALL, ⎫
DAVID FOSTER, ⎪
ISAAC CLARK, ⎬ *Committee.*
JOSIAH FISHER, ⎪
EBENEZER NIMS. ⎭

The Council that ordained Mr. Bacon, and organized the church, were " The Pastors and Delegates from the

* It is difficult to tell precisely what was the value of the Old Tenor at that date.

churches of Wrentham, Sunderland, Northfield, and Medway, viz.: Rev. Messrs. Messenger, Rand, Doolittle and Bucknam."

The following are the nineteen persons who then constituted the church, viz.:

JEREMIAH HALL,	JOSEPH ELLIS,
DAVID FOSTER,	JOSEPH RICHARDSON,
WILLIAM SMEED,	EBENEZER NIMS,
SETH HEATON,	JOSEPH GUILD,
NATHAN BLAKE,	EDWARD DALE,
JOSIAH FISHER,	SOLOMON RICHARDSON,
JOSEPH FISHER,	ABNER ELLIS,
JOHN BULLARD,	EBENEZER DAY,
OBADIAH BLAKE.	

David Foster and Josiah Fisher were appointed Deacons, at a church-meeting soon after the organization of the church.

The Rev. Mr. Bacon was a graduate of Harvard College in 1731. He continued a much-beloved pastor of this church, for nearly ten years; some were added to the Lord during his ministry, but the record was destroyed, at the time of the burning of the town by the Indians. Mr. Bacon was excused from all further obligation to the people, by an informal vote of the Proprietors, just before they abandoned the town.*

It was on the 10th of July, 1745, that the Indians began their depredations, by shooting Deacon Josiah Fisher, while driving his cow to pasture. And it soon became necessary for all the settlers to betake themselves to the fort, which was nearly on the site of the residence of the late Dr. C. G. Adams. Mrs. M'Kenny and Mr. John Bullard were killed April 23d, 1746; and Mr. Nathan

---

* This vote was taken on the common, in the haste of their departure.

Blake* was carried captive to Canada; and several buildings were burned. The people spent wretched days and nights, still living in the fort until the spring of 1747, when it was resolved to abandon the settlement. This resolution was carried into effect immediately; when the Indians set fire to the meeting-house, and all the other buildings except the mill on Beaver Brook, and the house of the miller; and Mr. Bacon was informally dismissed, as above remarked. He afterward resided, it is believed, in Old Rowley, Mass. The late venerable Thurston, of Maine, of blessed memory, was one of his descendants.

The town was forsaken for about three years. It is not known precisely when the settlers returned. But application was made April 11th, 1753, to Gov. Benning Wentworth, of New Hampshire, to procure a charter, which charter embraced the original limits of the Upper Ashuelot, and a small strip additional on the eastern side. Their corporation then received the name of Keene.†

It may not be amiss here, to record the fact, that as early as 1740, there was a contest between Massachusetts and New Hampshire, concerning the right of possession of the Valley of the Upper Ashuelot. The inhabitants settled it as a part of Massachusetts; and when it was decided that it belonged to New Hampshire, they presented "a petition to the King's Most Excellent Majesty,

---

* Nathan Blake was the grandfather of Mr. Abel Blake. He remained among the Indians about two years, and was held in high estimation as a chief. After his return to Keene he lived many years, and died in 1812, in the one hundredth year of his age.

† It is mentioned in *Hale's Annals,* that it is probable Gov. Wentworth named the place *"Keene"* in honor of Sir Benjamin Keene, who was Minister from England to Spain, about that time.

that they might be annexed to the Province of Massachusetts." They even appointed Thomas Hutchinson, Esq., to present their petition, who went to England for the purpose, but failed of accomplishing the object of his agency.*

The first meeting of the town, under the new charter, as KEENE, was in May, 1753. And then the regard of the people for religious order was shown by the erection of a meeting-house of slabs, on a green spot near to where Mr. Robert Stewart now resides.† This was for a temporary place of worship, until a more suitable house could be built. And in December of the same year, it was "voted to build a meeting-house 45 feet long, and 35 feet wide." It was at first resolved to place it near to where the Aaron Hall house now stands.‡ But it was finally erected on the south side of the Common. § That meeting-house was used till the autumn of 1786; when it was taken down, removed to the west side of the Common, and set up as the Court-House of Cheshire County. Fifty years ago, it was familiarly known as the " Old Court-House." This was, many years afterward, removed to Washington street; and a part of it is now the house of Capt. Pierce.

But to go back a little, in our history. It was in June, 1753, that Keene and the Lower Township on the Ashuelot River, (that is, Swanzey) united in giving the Rev. Ezra Carpenter, a call to settle in the work of the ministry. He was a graduate of Harvard College in 1720. He had before been settled in the Old Colony,

* Vide Hale's Annals, p. 16.
† Appleton House, Main st., opposite Marlborough st.
‡ Since removed, and given place to Mr. Henry Colony's house.
§ Nearly upon the site of the Soldiers' Monument.

and was a man of high character. His connection with Keene and Swanzey, continued seven years, both churches being one, until it was judged expedient for Mr. Carpenter to devote all his labors to Swanzey, and Keene sought another minister.

When Mr. Carpenter was installed over Keene and Swanzey, Oct. 4th, 1753, there were present, by their Elders, etc., the First Church in Hingham, the Third Church in Plymouth, the Church in Kingston in the County of Plymouth, the First Church in Lancaster, the Church in Nichewong, the Church in Poquoiag (Athol), the Church in Deerfield, the Church in Sunderland, and the Church in Northfield.*

During Mr. Carpenter's ministry, there were 52 baptisms of persons in Keene, and several were added to the church. But the record of the latter is lost. The above record of baptisms, was made by the Rev. Edward Goddard, "from the old book."

On June 11th, 1761, the Rev. Clement Sumner was ordained Pastor of this church. He was a graduate of Yale College in 1758, and his labors continued eleven years; when, in consequence of difficulties, he was dismissed, at his own request, by an ecclesiastical council.†

---

* Vide Records of Churches in Swanzey.

† It may not be uninteresting here to mention, that when Mr. Sumner was settled, his salary was fixed at thirty-five pounds sterling, and his firewood, with an annual increase of one pound ten shillings sterling, until fifteen pounds should be added

And be it here remarked, that his salary was estimated on commodities, as follows, viz. : wheat at 3s. 2½d. sterling ; pork 3d. per pound ; beef at 2d. per pound ; Indian corn at 1s. 8d. per bushel ; rye at 2s. 6d. per bushel ; labor at 2s. per day.

This was rescinded afterward, upon Mr. Sumner's suggesting that the article of beef was stated above the market price! What would he have thought, had it been stated as high as it is in 1868,—instead of two pence per pound ?

It was during his ministry, that the practice of " owning the covenant," as it was called, and having children baptized, was brought into use. Twenty persons thus owned the covenant, and seventy-three were added to full communion, during his ministry. But we have no record of baptisms by him. Mr. Sumner was never settled again; but he preached for a time in Thetford, Vt., and he died in Keene, March 29th, 1795.*

The following persons were members of this church at its re-organization (1761), under Mr. Sumner, viz.:

DAVID FOSTER,	EBENEZER DAY,
OBADIAH BLAKE,	JONAH FRENCH,
JOSIAH GUILD,	EPHRAIM DORMAN,
SETH HEATON,	NATHAN BLAKE,
MICHAEL METCALF,	JOHN SESSIONS,
EBENEZER NIMS,	JOSEPH ELLIS,
DAVID NIMS,	MICHAEL METCALF, JUN.

That is, *fourteen* male members. Their wives had probably not removed their relation from other churches, on account of the unsettled state of things. But we find that the following persons were received *by letter*, under Mr. Sumner, viz.:

JOHN DAY,	EXPERIENCE FISHER,
ABIEL DAY,	THANKFUL WILLARD,
DEBORAH GUILD,	GIDEON ELLIS,
THANKFUL HEATON,	URIAH WILSON AND WIFE,
ELIZABETH BLAKE,	SARAH BAKER,
EBENEZER CLARK,	SARAH WYMAN,
ANNA CLARK,	SARAH FOSTER,
ANNA METCALF,	MARY SANGER,
ELIZABETH SUMNER.	

That is, 4 males and 14 females.

---

* Rev. Mr. Sumner was buried in the old cemetery on the banks of Beaver Brook ; where his grave, with those of other worthy fathers of Keene, has been desecrated and forgotten. His widow survived him, some 25 years. She died about 1820, and was buried in West Swanzey. Dr. Barstow preached her funeral sermon, soon after his settlement in Keene.

And the following were admitted to full communion by profession, under Mr. Sumner, viz.:

MERCY ELLIS,	ABIGAIL NIMS,
SAMUEL HOLMES AND WIFE,	ELIPHALET CARPENTER,
ACHSA HALL,	MILLATIAH HALL,
WILLIAM WOODS AND WIFE,	JOSIAH ELLIS AND WIFE,
ESTHER GUILD,	ABIJAH METCALF,
ABIGAIL STILES,	ESTHER BLAKE,
TIMOTHY ELLIS,	BENJAMIN ARCHER AND WIFE,
ABIGAIL BRIGGS,	JEMIMA CLARK,
BENJAMIN OSGOOD AND WIFE,	PETER HAYWARD AND WIFE,
MRS. BALCH,	SARAH COOKE,
SAMUEL WOOD AND WIFE,	NATHANIEL KINGSBURY & WIFE,
GIDEON ELLIS, JUN., AND WIFE,	HANNAH WHEELER,
WILLIAM ELLIS,	SIMEON CLARK,
DANIEL KINGSBURY AND WIFE,	JESSE CLARK AND WIFE,
MILLATIAH CONLEY,	REUBEN DANIELS,
WILLIAM HOWARD AND WIFE,	THANKFUL POND,
EBENEZER KILBORN,	JESSE HALL,
HEPZIBAH DORMAN,	THOMAS WILDER AND WIFE,
ELISHA BRIGGS AND WIFE,	ELIZABETH BLAKE,
MISS HALL,	JONATHAN ARCHER,
SUSANNAH BALCH,	MARY WILLARD.

That is, 23 males and 33 females—or 56 in all.

And the following "owned the covenant," viz.:

DR. FRINK * AND WIFE,	HULDAH CLARK,
GIDEON ELLIS, JUN., AND WIFE,	MARY WILSON,
JOSEPH BROWN AND WIFE,	REBECCA WOODS,
SAMUEL WADSWORTH & WIFE,	LUTHER BRAGG AND WIFE,
ISAAC ESTY AND WIFE,	ABRAHAM WHEELER AND WIFE,
PHŒBE WADE,	ELIZABETH BRAGG,
	MARIA SWAN.

That is, 7 males and 13 females—or 20 in all. Eleven of these were afterward admitted to full communion.

The Covenant of the church under Mr. Sumner, embraced very nearly the same topics as our present Covenant. The Articles of Faith were thirteen, expressed in

* Father of "Polly" Frink.

part by the language of the Assembly's Cathechism, embodying the principal doctrines of the Reformation; and such were probably the original articles of the Church at its formation.

On the 2d of December, 1777, it was voted unanimously:—"To give Mr. Aaron Hall, (who has been labouring with us for some time,) a call to settle in the work of the ministry." Mr. Hall objected, "That he could not see his way clear to answer their call, unless the Church would reject the practice of persons owning the Covenant, to have their children baptized."

At length the church "voted unanimously, to reconsider the vote which permitted persons to offer their children in Baptism, who only owned the Covenant; and for the future, not to admit any upon this *half-way practice*, as it is called." It was also voted at the same meeting, "That whosoever belonging to this Church, shall have any objections against either the doctrines or conduct of his Pastor, shall, without dealing with him according to the rule given by our Blessed Lord, in Matthew 18th, concerning an offending Brother, or repair to another minister, or an officer in the Civil Law, or to any other person, to consult or concert measures against his Pastor: that such a conduct shall be looked upon as a breach of the order of the Gospel, and accordingly be proceeded against, in the Church. And the same shall be observed in regard to a private Brother." What confusion would have been avoided, had all that ever belonged to this church, followed this rule of conduct!

The difficulty of which Mr. Hall complained, being removed, he was ordained their Pastor, Feb. 18th, 1778. He was a graduate of Yale College in 1772; received his Master's degree in 1775, at Yale, and also at Dartmouth, in 1778. He had a long and happy, ministry; was universally respected, and died lamented, in the 63d year of his age, and the 37th of his ministry, August 12th, 1814. During his ministry, 211 were received into the church, and 871 were baptized.

The church consisted of 77 members when they renewed covenant, after abolishing " the half-way practice," preparatory to Mr. Hall's settlement, only five of the original members being then alive, viz.: David Foster, Seth Heaton, David Nims, Obadiah Blake and Nathan Blake.

When Mr. Hall was ordained, the Rev. Mr. Hibbard opened the solemnity by prayer; Rev. Mr. Olcott preached; Rev. Mr. Brigham, of Marlborough, made the ordaining prayer; Rev. Mr. Fessenden, of Walpole, gave the charge; Rev. Mr. Goddard gave the Right Hand of Fellowship, and the Rev. Mr. Sprague, of Dublin, closed the solemnity by prayer.*

It was during Mr. Hall's ministry, that our present meeting-house was built, viz., in the summer of 1786, and the two following years. It has since been twice remodeled.

It was no small work to build a meeting-house in those days, when money was scarce and transportation difficult. But resolution triumphed over difficulties. The inhabitants were divided into ten classes, and each class was assigned to some efficient man, to see that his class provided their proportion of materials for the building. The pews were sold *in anticipation* of doing the work, and paid for *in cattle*, at a certain appraise-

* Mr. Hall's salary was, at first £80, or $266.66; and it was increased from year to year, until it reached the amount of $500.

2

ment. But those cattle, after being driven to Wrentham, Boston, or other places, were sold at a great dis-
count. Besides, the difficulty of procuring lime, glass,
nails, and other necessary materials, was very great. Be it
remembered by all the young people of this community,
as a mark of England's oppression of these colonies, that
before the declaration of American Independence, the
colonies were not allowed to manufacture even a hob-
nail, to say nothing of other manufactures, that so all
might be dependent upon Old England for supplies.

The following charges of one of the Building Committee, may serve to give some idea of their difficulties, viz:

"To a journey, in Feb., 1787, to Sutton, Franklin,
and Boston, to purchase oil, glass, and vane—expense,
£1 4s."

"To a journey down with 97 head of Cattel to
Wrentham, Dec., 1787; also, to a journey to Providence,
to buy glass for meeting-house, and expence of keeping
said Cattel—£5 3s. 10d."

"May, 1788, to a journey down to Providence after the
glass, and carting glass from Providence to Wrentham,
also, a journey from Providence to Boston—£0 19s. 1d."

The following shows how exceedingly difficult it was
to procure Lawful money in those times, viz: "January
19th, 1787, voted, 1st, to hire one hundred pounds of
silver money toward finishing the meeting-house; and
2d, voted, that Deacon Daniel Kingsbury be appointed
to procure said money, *if possible.*" *

After the death of the Rev. Mr. Hall, the Rev. David

* The heads of the ten classes above-mentioned, were: 1. John Houghton;
2. Cornelius Sturtevant; 3. Joseph Blake; 4. Timothy Ellis; 5. Isaac Billings;
6. Daniel Guild; 7. Nathan Blake; 8. Benjamin Osgood; 9. ——— ———;
10. James Wright; and the Building Committee were Lieut. Benj. Hall,

Oliphant (a graduate of Union College in 1809,) was in-vited to preach as a candidate for settlement. He came in the autumn of 1814, about the time of the annual Thanksgiving. And he was ordained pastor of this church, May 24th, 1815.

There was not a union of the people in the settlement of Mr. Oliphant, and a remonstrance against it was presented by the minority. Yet the Council proceeded to his ordination. Rev. Mr. Dickinson, of Walpole, offered the first prayer; Rev. Mr. Hall, of New Ipswich, preached the sermon; Rev. Mr. Pratt, of Westmoreland, offered the ordaining prayer; Rev. Mr. Ainsworth, of Jaffrey, gave the Charge; Rev. Mr. Burge, of West Brattleboro', Vt., expressed the Fellowship; and Rev. Mr. Edwards, of Andover, Mass., offered the concluding prayer.

Under the administration of Mr. Oliphant, ninety-one were added to the church, and one hundred and twenty-nine were baptized. His ministry continued scarcely three years. But he made a deep impression upon many minds; and he will probably find many among this people, as the crown of his rejoicing in the day of the Lord Jesus.

It is unnecessary, here, to recount the difficulties which resulted in the dismission of Mr. Oliphant, in the autumn of 1817. He was soon settled as Pastor of the 3d church in Beverly, Mass., where he had a successful ministry of sixteen years. He was afterward installed over a church in the State of Maine. His present residence is Andover, Mass.*

Dea. Daniel Kingsbury, Major Davis Howlett, Lieut. Reuben Partridge, Mr. Abijah Wilder, Mr. Benj. Archer, and Mr. Thomas Baker. Their records and votes are in the hands of the Pastor.

* Mr. Oliphant died in 1872.

The speaker, a graduate of Yale College in 1813, came to this place Feb. 26th, 1818. He found the people so excited by the difficulties which arose concerning Mr. Oliphant, that he resolved to leave them, the moment that his first engagement had expired. And having been invited to another place,* he gave encouragement to that people that he would comply with their request, when his engagement in Keene had ended, if they were at peace among themselves. But such were the leadings of Providence, that he was constrained to abide here.

And he may be allowed to quote from the *N. H. Sentinel* of fifty years since, the following notice:

"ORDINATION.

"Keene, July 4th, 1818.

"On Wednesday last (1st inst.), Mr. Zedekiah S. Barstow was ordained to the Pastoral care of the Church and Congregation in this town. The Introductory prayer was made by Rev. Mr. Cooke, of Acworth; sermon by the Rev. Mr. Woodbridge, of Hadley, [Mass.], from Titus, 2d, 15th, 'Let no man despise thee;' consecrating prayer by the Rev. Mr. Fish, of Marlborough; Charge by Rev. Mr. Wood, of Chesterfield; Address to the Church and Congregation, by Rev. Dr. Thayer, of Lancaster [Mass.]; Right Hand of Fellowship, by the Rev. Mr. Crosby, of Charlestown; and the Concluding prayer, by Rev. Mr. Dickinson, of Walpole. Benediction by the Pastor.

"In the invitations of the Church and Society, and in all the subsequent measures relative to the settlement of Mr. Barstow, there has not been a dissenting vote. This harmony of action seems, and we trust will prove, but the harbinger of a pleasant and happy life to the Pastor, and of his usefulness in promoting the best interests of his numerous flock.

"The exercises were commenced by the choir performing the anthem, 'God is our hope and shield,' and closed with the anthem

* Topsfield, Mass.

by Williams, 'O praise the Lord,' and the Hallelujah Chorus by Dr. Miller."

It does not behoove the speaker to say much of himself, or of his manner of life among this people. But he has found work in abundance to be done; has preached more than 8500 sermons; has been invited to serve on 202 Ecclesiastical Councils; has married 560 couples; has performed 115 services at ordinations, installations, and dedications, of which, 48 were the preaching of the sermon.

During this pastorate, 782 members have been added to the church, if we include those now propounded; 838 have been baptized, and many to whom the speaker has ministered, are now scattered throughout the Union. Wherever he goes in the far West, he is accosted with many proofs of kindness and affection, by those who were once worshipers here.

During Mr. Oliphant's ministry, our Baptist brethren organized a church of 14 members in the west part of the town, to which the Rev. Messrs. Hale, Moore and Wheeler, successively ministered for a season. This church, however, disbanded about the year 1833. The Baptist church, now in existence here, was formed July 22d, 1832, under the name of the " Union Baptist Church of Keene." The title, " Union," however, was soon dropped. The majority of its constituent members were persons who had withdrawn from the old church. The two seem not to have been friendly to each other. But the trouble was soon ended by the extinction of the old church. The present church has had 415 members, of whom 181 have been added to it by baptism, and its present membership is 134. The first pastor was Rev.

C. G. Wheeler, who was ordained Aug. 21st, 1832. He remained, however, only about one year. The church seems to have had no pastor from Aug., 1833, to October, 1838. At that time Rev. John Peacock came, and supplied the pulpit somewhat more than a year. During his stay, the house of worship was built. It was dedicated Sept. 17th, 1839. Rev. Mark Carpenter became pastor in April, 1840, and remained until October, 1844. Rev. Horace Richardson was ordained pastor May 6th, 1845, and left in March, 1846. Rev. Gilbert Robbins was settled in July, 1846, and remained pastor until June, 1857. Rev. Leonard Tracy was pastor from Aug., 1857, to June, 1863. The Rev. W. N. Clark, the present pastor, began to supply the church in Sept., 1853, and was ordained, January 14th, 1854.

The Unitarian Congregational Society, of this place, was formed in the spring of 1824, and the church in connection with it was constituted Dec. 27th, 1825, consisting of 13 members. During the ministry of the Rev. Thomas Russell Sullivan, 64 were added to the church; during Rev. Abiel Abbott Livermore's ministry, 66; and during that of Rev. W. O. White, 90, making in all, 220 members.

Our Methodist brethren organized their communion in November, 1835, consisting of 30 members. Their numbers have greatly increased. At the present time they have 185 members, and since their church was first established, 300 have been added.

The Episcopal and Roman Catholic communions are prosperous, but the speaker has not succeeded in obtaining their precise satistics.

During October, 1867, one hundred and twenty-one of our members judged it expedient to colonize and form another Congregational church, under the impression that they could be more prosperous, than by continuing with us. Since that time, numbers have been added to their communion, and their present membership is about 160. But the history of this movement is so recent, and so well understood, that it is not necessary to enter upon it here.

During the fifty years of this pastorate, what changes have been witnessed in Keene! Fifty years ago, our church building stood in the middle of the common, facing Main street, and in rear of it was a long row of horse-sheds, beyond which, where now are so many beautiful dwellings, there was only a cow pasture. On Roxbury street, there is no house now standing that was then there, except that of Mr. Edwards, and a small one-story house beyond. On Court Street, upon the west side, were the houses of Mr. Prentiss, Mr. Tilden, Mrs. Elijah Parker, and what was then called the Old Sun Tavern. And on the east side, the house where the Rev. Mr. Karr resides, the house of Mr. Dodge, and the house where Deacon A. Wright died. All the rest are entirely new. The changes in the other streets, are equally great and impressive. And what changes have been witnessed among the inhabitants of the whole town! No less than 2,698 have passed to "that undiscovered country, from whose bourne no traveller returns." Only two* couples now live together in the family state, that were so living, fifty years since; and only one couple, in the house where they then lived.

And what progress has been made during the half-century, now closed, in science, literature, com-

* Alex. Grimes and wife, and Thos. Ellis and wife.

merce, manufactures and all the arts of life! What a multiplicity of inventions and discoveries; what improvements by the application of steam in the arts; in the modes of travelling; in the circulation of intelligence by the press, and by the magnetic telegraph! The inventor of the magnetic telegraph (Morse) was in college with the speaker. We took passage together in the first steamboat that plied the waters of Long Island Sound. The first journey of the speaker, from New Haven to Keene, occupied three days. It now requires but six or seven hours.

And other things have in an equal ratio, progressed throughout the civilized world. What pages of the world's strangest history have been written within the limits of this pastorate! When I first came to this valley, Napoleon the Great had just finished his wonderful career, and gone into exile at St. Helena, that rock of the ocean, where he died three years afterward. Louis XVIII. sat on the throne of France, as the representative of the restored house of the Bourbons. Three revolutions have since occurred in regard to that throne. Pius VII. wore the Papal Tiara, though degraded by Napoleon, and held in less honor than his predecessors. George III. of England still lingered in imbecility in his bed-chamber, while the Prince Regent waited impatiently for the death of his father, which should give him the throne of Great Britain, with the title of George IV. James Monroe had passed one year of his first term of office as President of the United States. Jefferson and the elder Adams, Madison and Jay, and their noble compeers, were still alive. Only twenty States then constituted our Republic, with scarcely nine millions of inhabitants. As many more States have since been added, with three times as many millions of square miles; and the population of the republic has been quadrupled! "The West" was then *terra incognita;* and the vast region beyond the Mississippi, where now the iron horse ranges more than 640 miles, was described in the school-boy's Atlas, as "unexplored territory."

Mexico, in the meantime, has passed through eight changes of constitutional liberty, anarchy, and misrule. And what changes have been wrought in Italy, Austria, Prussia, and the Papal States!

All, surely, will acknowledge that it has been an eventful half century; in that it has revolutionized nations; extended the Scriptures in almost two hundred languages and dialects of men; and opened nearly all the nations of the earth, for the introduction of the glorious Gospel of the Blessed God!

And now, what has the speaker to regret, but that he has done so little in comparison with what he wished to do, to bring men to the Saviour, and to give the king-dom to the Son of God! And in closing his ministry, he earnestly beseeches all whom he has ever addressed on the high concerns of their immortal interests, to give diligence that they may be found of God in peace. Do, now, consider these forcible words of the poet:

———"Oh! what is time?"
I asked an aged man, a man of cares,
Wrinkled, and curved, and white with hoary hairs.
"Time is the warp of life," he said; "O tell
The young, the fair, the gay, to weave it well!"

I asked a dying sinner, ere the stroke
Of ruthless Death, life's golden bowl had broke;
I asked *him,* "What is time?" "*Time?*" he replied,
"*I've lost it!* Ah, the treasure!" And he died!

With this discourse, my dear friends, I close the half century of my pastorate. Resigning altogether, herewith, the active duties of the ministry, commending you to God, and the word of His grace, and committing this beloved flock to the care of my much-esteemed successor,* I seek that repose which is due to infirmity and to age; not indeed that I shall ever cease to care for your welfare, but in no meddlesome mood, when released from the absorbing cares of a shepherd of the flock. I little thought, when, just fifty years ago this morning, I stood up here, a young man, a novice in the ministry, to be set apart to the life-service of the Master, that my entire ministerial life would be passed among the same people, and that it would end where it began, at the close of half a century. But God, in His wise and merciful providence, has so ordered it. And now, after an experience so long and so varied, as shepherd of this flock, the same still, though changed by the vicissitudes of nearly two generations, having baptized and married parents, and their children, and their grand-children; I again stand before you to-day, to say:

Beloved Friends, Farewell! And may the God of Peace dwell in you, and bless you evermore!

* The Rev. W. S. Karr.

ORDER OF EXERCISES

AT

THE 1st CONGREGATIONAL CHURCH, KEENE, N. H., JULY 1, 1868,

ON THE OCCASION OF

THE FIFTIETH ANNIVERSARY OF THE ORDINATION OF THE

REV. Z. S. BARSTOW, D.D.

———••———

1. **ANTHEM,**
    By the CHOIR.

2. **INTRODUCTORY PRAYER,**
    By REV. J. ORCUTT, D.D., *of N. Y. City.*

3. **READING OF THE SCRIPTURES,**
    By PROF. HENRY E. PARKER, *of Dartmouth College.*

4. **PRAYER,**
    By REV. DR. BOUTON, *of Concord, N. H.*

5. **PSALM 90,**
    "O God! Our help in ages past,"
    By the CHOIR.

6. **DISCOURSE,**
    By REV. DR. BARSTOW.

7. **CLOSING PRAYER,**
    By REV. W. S. KARR, *of Keene.*

8. **ANTHEM,**
    By the CHOIR.

9. **BENEDICTION,**
    By REV. MR. GAYLORD, *of Nashua.*

NOTE.

The exercises at the church, were followed by a Public Dinner, given to Dr. Barstow, at the Town Hall. by the citizens of Keene. All denominations were represented at the table ; the attendance was very large, and the exercises, consisting of sentiments and speeches, were of the most interesting character. It is to be regretted, that, as the occasion was one so intimately connected with the history of the Town, for a period of fifty years, no provision was made at the time for securing a complete and a permanent record of the proceedings, beyond the brief sketches which appeared in the newspapers of the day.

1738.

MANUAL

OF THE

First Congregational Church,

KEENE, N. H.

1877.

Historical Sketch,

ARTICLES OF FAITH AND COVENANT,

AND

REGULATIONS

OF THE

First Congregational Church,

KEENE, N. H.,

WITH

LIST OF MEMBERS.

KEENE:
SENTINEL PRINTING COMPANY, BOOK AND JOB PRINTERS.
1877.

HISTORICAL SKETCH.

THE history of the First Congregational Church of Keene is closely interwoven with that of the Town.

Its origin dates back to the old colonial days. Oct. 18, 1738, a church was organized in Upper Ashuelot, as the settlement was first called, and "the worthy Jacob Bacon" ordained its pastor. Mr. Bacon remained with his people until the settlement was abandoned, on account of the Indian difficulties, in 1747. With the coming of more quiet times, the settlers returnèd, and the church was re-established.

From 1753 to 1760 the people of Keene and Swanzey worshiped together, under the pastorate of Rev. Mr. Carpenter.

The Keene church was reorganized in 1761, and Mr. Clement Sumner was then ordained, who remained with them till 1772, when he was dismissed.

For six years the church was without a pastor. Rev. Aaron Hall, for thirty-seven years "the beloved and popular minister of Keene," was ordained Feb. 18, 1778, and during his ministry two hundred and eleven members were received to the church.

The new meeting house, which stood about seventy feet south of its present location, was dedicated Oct. 4, 1738.

Rev. David Oliphant succeeded Mr. Hall, and was ordained May 24, 1815. During his ministry of three years, ninety-one united with the church.

Rev. Zedekiah S. Barstow was installed July 1, 1818. During the period of Dr. Barstow's settlement, the church edifice was twice repaired and re-dedicated: once in 1829, when it was moved to its present location ; and again in 1860, when it became the building we of to-day know.

Until 1861, Dr. Barstow performed all the labors of his pastorate alone ; but advancing age, and the increasing size of the church and society, called for an assistant. His first colleague, Rev. J. A. Hamilton, was installed in 1861, and at his own request dismissed in 1865.

Soon after, Rev. J. A. Leach was called as a colleague. In 1867 the church divided, and a part, with Rev. Mr. Leach as pastor, organized as the Second Congregational Church.

After an active pastorate of fifty years, in 1868, Dr. Barstow resigned his charge ; and the first Sunday in March, 1873, just fifty-five years from the day he first preached in Keene, he breathed his last. The feeling his death caused is well expressed in the words of his funeral sermon, delivered by Prof. Parker of Dartmouth College, a former member of this church : " What truer epitome of his life can we give, what fitter eulogy utter, than to pronounce. as we never did before, what the Apostle gives as the delineation of such, forever : readiness to be offered—the time of departure at hand—a good fight fought—the Christian race finished—the faith kept—a coronation at the hand of God—a crown of righteousness at the world's assize,—all his !"

Rev. W. S. Karr was installed soon after Dr. Barstow's fiftieth anniversary. In December, 1872, to the regret of his people, Mr. Karr resigned, to accept the call of the Prospect Street Church, Cambridgeport, Mass.

The present pastor, Rev. Cyrus Richardson, was installed July 10, 1873.

During its existence of one hundred and forty years, the church has had eight pastors and two associate pastors.

CONFESSION OF FAITH.

As a Church of Jesus Christ, associated in accordance with the teachings of the New Testament, for the public worship of God, for the observance of Gospel sacraments and ordinances, for mutual edification and encouragement in the Christian life, and for the advancement of the Redeemer's Kingdom, we declare our union in Faith and Love with all who love our Lord Jesus Christ. Receiving the Scriptures of the Old and New Testaments as the Word of God, and the only infallible rule of religious faith and practice, we confess our faith in the one living and true God, revealed as the Father, the Son, and the Holy Ghost; the Creator and Preserver of all things, whose purposes and providence extend to all events, and who exercises a righteous government over all his creatures.

We believe in the universal sinfulness and ruin of our race : since " By one man sin entered into the world. and death by sin ; and so death passed upon all men, for that all have sinned."

We believe that the Lord Jesus Christ, the Son of God, having taken upon himself our nature, has, by his obedience, sufferings, and death, provided a way of salvation for all mankind : and that, through faith in his name, whosoever will may be saved.

We believe that, although salvation is offered freely to all, they only repent and believe in Christ, who, in thus obeying the Gospel, are regenerated by the Holy Spirit ; and that all who are thus regenerated are " kept by the power of God, through faith, unto salvation."

We believe that the Christian Sabbath, the Ministry of the Word, the Visible Church, and the Ordinances of Baptism and the Lord's Supper, are divinely appointed, and are binding on the followers of Christ until his coming.

We believe that there is a day appointed, in which God will raise the dead, and judge the world ; that the wicked shall "go away into everlasting punishment, and the righteous into life eternal."

Do you thus solemnly profess to believe?

BAPTISM.

[The Pastor will first address those who come by profession, and who have been baptized in infancy, as follows :]

You who were dedicated to God in your childhood in the ordinance of Infant Baptism, by your believing parents, do hereby declare your personal acceptance of the same, and your belief that the regeneration hereby signified has been wrought within your soul by the Holy Spirit.

[Then to the others the Pastor will say :]

You, who trust that your hearts have been renewed by the Holy Spirit, but who have never received the outward seal of the covenant, will now, upon this profession of your faith, present yourselves for the ordinance of Baptism.

[When Baptism has been administered, the Pastor will then say :]

Attend, now, to the covenants into which you are to enter with God and this Church.

COVENANT.

You who now present yourselves to be received into our fellowship do, by this act, avow your personal sense of the love of God in the forgiveness of your sins; and, trusting that He who hears and answers prayer will uphold and strengthen you, you do give yourselves to the Lord Jesus Christ, and covenant to be His disciples, receiving Him as your only Priest and Propitiation, your great Teacher, Lawgiver, and King; you dedicate yourselves to God as the object of your highest love, and to His service as your highest joy; engaging to walk with us in the due observance of Christian ordinances; and that, by the aid of the Divine Spirit, you will honor your profession by a constant Christian life.

Do you thus covenant with God and with this church?

[Here the members of the church will stand up, and the Pastor will read the following :]

RESPONSE OF THE CHURCH.

We, then, the members of this church, in view of these your professions and engagements, do joyfully and affectionately receive you to this communion, and welcome you to this fellowship with us in the blessings of the Gospel and in service of our Divine Redeemer.

We covenant to love and watch over you, and in Christian fidelity to seek your advancement in the life and likeness of him whose name we bear.

And now, beloved of the Lord, let it be impressed upon your minds that you have entered into solemn engagements, from which you can never escape.

Wherever you go, these vows will be upon you. They will follow you to the bar of God, and abide upon you to eternity. May you walk worthy of God, and of your profession ! May the Lord guide and preserve you till death ; and at last receive you and us to that blessed world, where our love and joy shall be forever perfect ! And unto Him who is able to keep us from falling, and to present us faultless before the presence of His glory with exceeding joy, to the only wise God, our Saviour, be glory and majesty, dominion and power, both now and forever. Amen.

[Here the Pastor may give the Right Hand to each person, with such words as he may be pleased to add.]

PRINCIPLES AND RULES.

ARTICLE I.—NAME.

This Church shall be called the FIRST CONGREGATIONAL Church of Keene, N. H.

ARTICLE II.—GOVERNMENT.

SEC. 1.—We hold that all ecclesiastical authority is vested in the local church, which has power to choose its own pastor, elect its own officers, make its own regulations, and conduct its own affairs in general, recognizing as its head only the Lord Jesus Christ.

At the same time we gladly enter into fellowship with other Christian churches of the same order, and consider ourselves bound to seek and expect advice from ecclesiastical councils in the more important affairs of church government.

ARTICLE III.—OFFICERS.

SEC. 1.—The officers of this church shall be a pastor, four deacons, three deaconesses, a clerk, a treasurer, auditor and examining committee, consisting of the pastor, deacons and three other members ; the deacons to be chosen for four years, the deaconesses three, so that the time of office of one shall expire each year ; the clerk, treasurer, auditor and examining committee to be elected annually.

SEC. 2.—The deacons shall provide for the communion table ; shall pass the bread and wine at the celebration of the Lord's Supper ; shall distribute the funds for the needy members ; and shall aid the pastor in keeping a spiritual oversight of the individual members of the church, and in organizing them into active labor for the sick, the poor, and the strangers in the parish ; in arranging annually a schedule for benevolent contribution ; in deciding in regard to notices to be read from the pulpit, which may seem to the pastor of doubtful propriety: and in all other matters which pertain to the spiritual welfare of the church.

SEC. 3.   DEACONESSES.—It shall be the duty of the deaconesses to see that the sick, the afflicted, the destitute, and the thoughtful, are visited either by themselves or by other members of the church ; to look after strangers who come among us, and see that they are introduced ; to make inquiries in cases of discipline of sisters ; to secure helpers in any work that falls to them by virtue of their office ; and in general to assist the pastor and deacons in organizing the members of the church into active service in the cause of the Master.

SEC. 4.—It shall be the duty of the clerk to keep an accurate record of all the business meetings of the church ; to conduct correspondence, keep on file important communications and official reports, and all other valuable papers of the church ; to notify officers, committees and delegates of their election or appointment, and to make a full report at the annual meeting.

SEC. 5.—It shall be the duty of the treasurer to receive and forward benevolent collections to the different objects for which they are contributed, requiring vouchers for the same, and to present a full report at the annual meeting.

SEC. 6.—It shall be the duty of the auditor to audit the accounts of the treasurer previous to the annual meeting.

SEC. 7.—It shall be the duty of the examining committee to examine all persons who propose to unite with the church either by profession of their faith or by letter, and to present to the church the names of those whom they approve. They shall act as a committee of preliminary inquiry in all cases of discipline. They shall make a report to the church of its condition and doings, with a list of all absent members, at the annual meeting.

ARTICLE IV.—MEMBERSHIP.

SEC. 1.—Persons who desire to unite with this church on profession of their faith, shall present their names to the examining committee, give credible evidence of Christian

2

character and personal piety, and, if approved by the committee, they shall be propounded before the congregation two weeks previous to the communion ; and if approved by a vote of the church at the time of the preparatory lecture, they shall be received into the church the following Sabbath, by publicly assenting to the articles of faith and covenant.

SEC. 2.—Persons bringing letters from other evangelical churches shall come before the committee, and, if approved, their letter shall be read before the congregation at least one week previous to admission. If received by vote of the church, at the preparatory lecture, they shall publicly assent to the articles of faith and covenant at the following communion.

SEC. 3.—Members of other churches who worship with us for more than one year, are expected to bring letters, unless there be special reasons for delay. A letter dated more than a year previous to its presentation will not be considered valid, without satisfactory explanation.

SEC. 4.—Members of this church who remove to other places where churches of like faith exist, are expected to take letters from this church within one year from their removal, unless they can give sufficient reason for delay. Letters of dismission are valid for one year only from their date.

ARTICLE V.—DISCIPLINE.

SEC. 1.—This church will endeavor to follow the law of Christ, as recorded in Matt. XVIII, 15–17, in cases of private offence among its members ; and in all disciplinary processes will carry out the spirit of this law.

SEC. 2.—Any member accused before the church shall be properly notified of the charge preferred against him, and an opportunity given him for making his defence. If brought to trial by the church, he shall personally be furnished with a written copy of the charges, and the names of the witnesses relied on for proof. The confession of the accused, or the testimony of two witnesses, or that which is fairly equivalent, shall be requisite for conviction. If the accused fail to appear at the trial, some member of the church shall be appointed to defend his case.

SEC. 3.—Every vote and sentence of excommunication shall be read before a regular meeting of the church.

SEC. 4.—An excommunicated person may, upon evidence of repentance, confession of sin, and reformation of his conduct, be readmitted to the church on profession.

ARTICLE VI.

SEC. 1.—The ordinance of the Lord's Supper shall be observed the first Sabbath afternoon in January, March, May, July, September, and November.

SEC. 2.—The regular meeting of the church for devotional services shall be held on Wednesday evenings. The meetings for preparatory lecture shall be held half of the time in the afternoon, and half of the time in the evening.

SEC. 3.—Other devotional meetings shall be appointed by the examining committee, as in their judgment the cause of Christ demands.

SEC. 4.—The annual business meeting shall be held in connection with the Wednesday evening devotional meeting following the communion Sabbath in September, at which time officers and committees of the church shall be chosen for the ensuing year or term. But any vacancy that occurs during the year may be filled at any regular meeting of the church, provided not less than twenty-five members shall be present, which number shall constitute a quorum for business; all members, male and female, being entitled and expected to vote; and all elections shall be determined by a majority of the members present and voting.

ARTICLE VII.—AMENDMENTS.

SEC. 1.—This Constitution, the Confession of Faith, and the Covenant, may be altered at a meeting, of which due notice shall be given on the two preceding Sabbaths, with a statement of the proposed alteration, by a majority of the members present and voting, provided the change does not infringe upon the doctrines or organic principles of this church.

SEC. 2.—By-laws to carry out the provisions of this constitution, may be enacted at any business meeting.

Names of Pastors from the Organization of the Church to the present time.

	NAMES.	SETTLEMENTS.	DATE.	DISMISSIONS.	DATE.
1	Jacob Bacon,	Installed,	Oct. 1738.	Town burned and deserted.	A. D. 1747.
2	Ezra Carpenter,	"	Oct. 1753.	Dismissed,	A. D. 1761.
3	Clement Sumner,	"	June 1761.	"	A. D. 1772.
4	Aaron Hall,	"	Feb. 1778.	Died in Keene, N. H.,	Aug. 1814.
5	David Oliphant,	"	May 1815.	Dismissed,	Nov. 1817.
6	Zedekiah S. Barstow,	"	July 1818.	Died in Keene, N. H.,	Mar. 1873.
7	John A. Hamilton,	"	Jan. 1851.	Dismissed,	Sept. 1865.
8	Joseph A. Leach,	"	July 1866.	"	Oct. 1867.
9	William S. Karr,	"	July 1868.	"	Dec. 1872.
10	Cyrus Richardson,	"	July 1873.	Present Pastor, -	

Names of Deacons from the Organization of the Church to the present time.

	NAMES.	INDUCTIONS.	DATE.	DISMISSIONS.	DATE.
1	Charles D. Foster,	Chosen,	Oct. 1738.	Died in Keene, N. H., before	A. D. 1818.
2	Josiah Fisher,	"	Oct. 1738.	" " "	A. D. 1818.
3	Obadiah Blake,	"	June 1763.	" " "	A. D. 1818.
4	Simeon Clark,	"	Jan. 1780.	" " "	A. D. 1818.
5	Daniel Kingsbury,	"	May 1780.	Died in Keene, N. H.,	Aug. 1825.
6	Abijah Wilder,	"	Mar. 1787.	" "	Jan. 1835.
7	Elijah Carter,	"	Oct. 1816.	" "	Feb. 1835.
8	Thomas Fisher,	"	Oct. 1816.	" "	Dec. 1834.
9	Collins H. Jaquith,	"	Dec. 1824.	Dismissed,	April 1840.
10	John W. Briggs,	"	Feb. 1832.	Died in Keene, N. H.,	Sept. 1839.
11	John W. Binney,	"	May 1832.	Dismissed,	June 1862.
12	Henry G. Perkins,	"	Nov. 1832.	"	Aug. 1834.
13	Christopher C. Denny,	"	Jan. 1840.	"	July 1846.
14	Isaac Rand,	"	Jan. 1840.	"	Oct. 1867.
15	Stewart Hastings,	"	Jan. 1840.	"	April 1861.
16	Asa Duren,	"	July 1861.	"	Oct. 1867.
17	George P. Drown,	"	July 1861.	"	Oct. 1867.
18	Elisha Rand,	"	Nov. 1865.	"	Oct. 1867.
19	Charles Bridgman,	"	Jan. 1868.	Present Deacon,	
20	Asa Maynard,	"	Jan. 1868.	Died in Keene, N. H.,	Sept. 1872.
21	William Metcalf,	"	Jan. 1868.	Present Deacon,	
22	Charles Keyes,	"	Jan. 1868.	Died in Keene, N. H.,	May 1874.
23	Charles H. Whitney,	"	April 1876.	Present Deacon.	
24	Charles W. Hyde,	"	April 1876.	Present Deacon,	

ROLL OF MEMBERSHIP,

The following Roll of Membership goes back a quarter of a century, including the names of all who were members in the year 1851, together with those (except excommunicated members) who have united since, up to March, 1877.

No.	Names.	How Admitted.	Date.	Dismissions.	Date.
1	Lucy Abbot	Letter from church in Surry, N H	Jan. 1834	To church in Surry, N H	Aug. 1860
2	Elijah Adams	Profession of faith	Nov. 1831	Med in Keene, N H	Dec. 1862
3	Amanda Adams	"	Jan. 1832	Died in Swanzey, "	July 1873
4	Daniel Adams	Letter from church in Mt Vernon	Nov. 1846	Died in Keene, "	June 1864
5	Nancy Adams	Profession of faith	May 1851		May 1851
6	Daniel E. Adams	"	Sept. 1852	Pastor in Wilton, N H	Dec. 1860
7	Ellen F. (Kingsbury) Adams	"	May 1850	To church in Wilton, N H	"
8	Mary Ann Adams	"	Nov. 1831	Present member	
9	John G. Adams	"	Nov. 1849	To church in St Charles, Ill	April 1858
10	William H. Adams	Letter from church in Pomfret, Vt.	Sept. 1846	To 2d church, Keene	Oct. 1847
11	Martha (Wallace) Adams	Letter from church in Westminster, Vt.	Dec. 1853	To church in Acworth, N II	June 1858
12	Emma A. Adams	Profession of faith	Nov. 1866	To 2d church, Keene	Oct. 1867
13	Holland H. Albee	Letter from church in Bernardston, Mass	Jan. 1870	Present member	
14	Maria W. (Spencer) Albee	Letter from church in Springfield, Vt	Nov. 1875	"	
15	George Allen	Profession of faith	Nov. 1845	To 2d church, Keene	Oct. 1867
16	Nancy R. Allen	"		Present member	
17	Susan (Wood) Allen	"	Nov. 1851	Present member	
18	Hannah W. Atwood	Letter from church in Nashua, N II	Jan. 1861	Lives near Nelson	
19	Nancy Ayer	Letter from church in Quincy, Mass	Nov. 1865	Present member	
	B.				
20	Jerusha Babbitt	Letter from church in Westmoreland, N II	Aug. 1831	Died in Keene	Jan. 1866
21	Amanda H. Baker	Profession of faith	May 1841	Present member	
22	Emily F. Baker	"	May 1862	"	
23	Ellen E. (Goodnow) Bancroft	"	Sept. 1855	"	
24	Ann A. Barker	Letter from church in Antrim, N H	Aug. 1870	To church in Somerville, Mass	Dec. 1873
25	Sally Barker	Letter from church in Marlborough, N H	Oct. 1823	To church in Bellows Falls, Vt.	Feb. 1855
26	Susanna Barker	Letter from church in Marlborough, N II	Mar. 1846	Returned to Marlborough, N H	Mar. 1873
27	Zedekiah S. Barstow, D. D.	Letter to Yale college, Ct	July 1818	Died in Keene	
28	Elizabeth F. Barstow	Letter from church in Westboro', Mass	Dec. 1818	Present member	Sept. 1869
29	Maria F. Barrett	Profession of faith	Mar. 1876	Present member	
30	Harriet Bassett	"	Jan. 1832	To church in Massillon, O	
31	Anna Batchelder	Member before	A. D. 1818	Died in Elktown, Pa	Aug. 1853
32	Hannah Batchelder	Letter from church in Roxbury, N H	May 1840	Died in Keene	Oct. 1864

	Name	How admitted	Date	Disposition	Date
33	John A. Batchelder	Letter from church in Swanzey, N H	Oct. 1862	Present member	
34	Elmina R. Batchelder	Profession of faith	Jan. 1871	"	
35	Clara L. Batchelder	"	Aug. 1870	Died in Keene	Mar. 1871
36	Joseph Beal	"	Jan. 1875	Present member	
37	Lois W. Beal	"			
38	Mary J. Beckley	Letter from church in Chesterfield, N H	Jan. 1875		
39	Mary E. (Skinner) Beckwith	Profession of faith	June 1866	To church in Honolulu, Sandwich Is	Dec. 1875
40	Harlan A. Bemis	Profession of faith	July 1866	Died in Vermont	Aug. 1872
41	Henry E. B. Betts	Letter from church in New York City	Mar. 1852	To church in New York city	Jan. 1854
42	Lucy O. (Kingsbury) Betts	Profession of faith	Jan. 1851		
43	Albert S. Bigelow	Letter from church in Swanzey, N H	May, 1864	To church in Greenfield, Mass	May, 1867
44	Lydia M. Bigelow	"			
45	Fanny (Whitcomb) Bigelow	Profession of faith	Sept. 1861	To Baptist church in Brooklyn, N Y	Mar. 1870
46	John W. Binney	Letter from church in Rindge, N H	Oct. 1828	Died in Keene	une 1862
47	Susan Binney	"			April 1865
48	Hannah T. Blake	Profession of faith	Jan. 1869	Present member	July 1860
49	Betsey Blake	"	Jan. 1836	Died in Keene	Sept. 1874
50	Mary R. Blake	"	Nov. 1882	"	Apr. 1872
51	Sarah J. (Hurd) Blake	"	Nov. 1881	To church in Cambridge, Mass	Apr. 1883
52	Sally Blake	Letter from church in Concord, Vt	May 1830	Died in Keene	May, 1874
53	Ada M. (Porter) Bodwell	Profession of faith	Jan. 1870	Present member	
54	Susan (Lamson) Boice	Letter from church in New London, Conn	Sept. 1845	Died in Keene	
55	Lauretta M. Boice	Profession of faith	1885	Present member	
56	Phebe P. Bolster	Letter from church in Jaffrey, N H	July 1876	"	
57	Solomon H. Brackett	Letter from church in Stoneham, Mass	July 1864	To church in St Johnsbury, Vt	Feb. 1876
58	Mary A. Brackett	Letter from church in Claremont, N H	Aug. 1860	Non-resident before	Sept. 1885
59	Adeline R. Bradford	Profession of faith	July 1876	Present member	
60	Samuel W. Bradford	Letter from church in Walpole, N H	May 1876	Died in Keene	
61	Sarah G. Bradford	Letter from church in Essex, N Y	May 1871	Died in Keene	June 1874
62	Sarah L. Brainard	Letter from church in Westminster, Vt	May, 1867	To 2d church, Keene	Oct. 1867
63	Orison E. Bragg	Letter from church in Gilsum, N H	Mar. 1862	To church in Chester, Vt	April 1867
64	Harriet M. Bragg	Profession of faith	Mar. 1859	Lives in Coleville, N Y	
65	Eliza Bragg	Letter from church in Sullivan, N H	July 1859	To church in Atchison, Kan	Dec. 1860
66	Mary Breed	Profession of faith	Sept. 1863	To Baptist church in Springfield, Mass	June 1871
67	German N. Breed	"	Jan. 1875	Lives in Worcester, Mass	
68	Ellen M. (Thompson) Brewer	Letter from church in Oswego, N Y	July 1813		
69	Helen F. (Guild) Brick	Letter from Baptist church, Keene	Mar. 1870	Present member	
70	Charles Bridgman	Profession of faith	July 1875	"	
71	Sarah H. Bridgman	"	Jan. 1836	To Park street church, Boston, Mass	Feb. 1853
72	Gertrude H. Bridgman	Letter from church in Fitzwilliam, N H	Dec. 1886	"	
73	Lucius D. Briggs				
74	Elizabeth H. Briggs				

No.	NAMES.	HOW ADMITTED.	DATE.	DISMISSIONS.	DATE.
73	Mary L. Briggs	Letter from church in Lockport, N Y	July 1-68	Present member	
76	Elizabeth S. Briggs	Profession of faith	Mar. 1837	To church in Chicago, Ill	Oct. 1853
77	John K. Briggs	Letter from Baptist church, Keene	Feb. 1872	Present member	
78	Lydia A. Briggs	Letter from church in Meredith, N H	Jan. 1869	"	
79	Mary C. Briggs	Profession of faith	May 1875		
80	Sally Briggs		Sept. 1833	Died in Keene	May 1851
81	Nancy Brooks	Letter from church in Roxbury, N H	Nov. 1826		Jan. 1867
82	William H. Brooks	Profession of faith	May, 1-66	To 2d church, Keene	Oct. 1867
83	Sarah L. Brooks	"		"	
84	Henry O. Brooks		July, 1866		
85	Sarah M. J. Brooks				
86	Cassandana Brown	Letter from Baptist church, Keene	July 1844	To church in Winchendon, Mass	Jan 1877
87	Ellen J. Brown	Letter from church in Sullivan, N H	June 1846	To 2d church, Keene	Oct. 1801
88	Frances Brown	Letter from church in Philadelphia, Pa	Nov. 185x	Died in Concord, N H	
89	Peter D. Buckminster	Letter from church in Roxbury, N H	July 1856	Died in Keene	Dec. 1873
90	Abigail W. Buckminster	"	"	"	Sept. 1878
91	Sarah J. Buckminster	"	"	"	July 1870
92	Emily E. (Buxton) Buckminster	Letter from 2d church, Keene	Jan. 1877	Present member	
93	Harriet I. Buckminster	Profession of faith	Mar. 1855	"	
94	Charles W. Buckminster	"	May 1871	"	
95	Addie I. Buffum	"	Mar. 1876	"	
96	Clara Bugbee	Letter from church in Hartford, Vt	Mar. 1870	Non-resident member	
97	Mary Bundy	Letter from church in Westminster, Vt	Jan. 1-55	Died in Keene	Dec. 1868
98	Sarah E. Burgess	Letter from church in Westboro', Mass	Mar. 1870	Present member	
99	Harriet Burnap	Letter from church in Nelson, N H	Mar. 1868	"	
100	Wellington R. Burton	Profession of faith	July 1876	"	
101	Mary H. Russ	"	Jan. 1869	"	
102	Mary E. Russ				
103	George A. Butterfield		Sept. 1856	With Baptist church in Chelsea, Mass	June 1876
104	Charlotte Butterfield			To Park street church, Boston, Mass	June 1864
105	Caroline S. Butterfield	Letter from church in Westmoreland, N H	Dec. "	Died in Keene	Jan. 1864
				Present member	

C.

No.	NAMES.	HOW ADMITTED.	DATE.	DISMISSIONS.	DATE.
106	David R. Calef	Profession of faith	Nov. 1888	Present member	
107	Zeuriah Carleton	Letter from church in Westmoreland, N H	June 1837	To church in Wilton, N H	Sept. 1851
108	William P. Carleton	Profession of faith	July 1876	Present member	
109	Clara H. Carpenter	"	May 1859	To Baptist church, Keene	June 1865
110	Dolly Chamberlain	Letter from church in Worcester, Mass	Jan. 1813	Present member	
111	Josephine E. Chaplin	Letter from church in Springfield, Ill	Oct. 1869	To church in Brooklyn, N Y	June 1875

No.	Name	Admission	Date	Status	Date
112	Lola Chapman	Profession of faith	Sept. 1843	Present member	
113	Maria E. Chapman	Letter from church in Oberlin, O.	Jan. 1865	To 2d church, Keene	Oct. 1867
114	Erastus Chase	Profession of faith	May 1831	Died in Keene	April 1874
115	Mary Chase	"	July 1831	Lives in Sandwich Islands	
116	Charles Chase	"	Sept. 1834	Died in Keene	Aug. 1866
117	Hannah Chase	Letter from church in Athol, Mass	May 1861	Present member	
118	Alfred Chase	Profession of faith	Jan. 1863	To church in Nashua, N H	June 1869
119	Jennie (Noble) Chase	"	May 1851	Died in Keene	
120	Eadie Chase	Letter from church in Chesterfield, N H	Nov. 1871	To church in Deerfield, Mass	June 1873
121	George H. Chase	Letter from church in Lempster, N H	Sept. 1876	To church in Deerfield, Mass	Oct. 1872
122	Joseph Chase	Profession of faith	July 1876	Present member	
123	Victoria B. Chase	Letter from Episcopal church, Keene	Feb. 1850	To church in South Boston, Mass	Dec. 1869
124	Albert Church	Letter from church in Hinsdale, N H			
125	Ellen M. Church				
126	Eunice Clark	Member before	A.D. 1818	Died in Keene	
127	Gideon Clark	Profession of faith	Jan. 1832	"	April 1875
128	Deben W. Clark	"	May 1820	"	Sept. 1859
129	Cornelia F. Clark	Letter from church in Swanzey, N H	June 1871	Present member	Oct. 1867
130	Edwin H. Clark	Letter from church in Greenfield, Mass	Jan. 1869	"	
131	Fanny M. Clark	Profession of faith			
132	Frances S. Colony	"	Sept. 1837	Died in Keene	Aug. 1876
133	Sarah R. Colony	"	July 1858	Present member	
134	Eunice J. Colony	"	July 1870	"	
135	Sarah E. (Chase) Converse	"	July 1-04	To M E church, Hartford, Ct	
136	Noah R. Cook	"	Mar. 1831	To 2d church, Keene	Jan. 1868 / Oct. 1867
137	Maria L. Cook				
138	Silas P. Cook	Letter from church in Walpole, N H	July 1841		
139	Mary C. (Foster) Cook	Profession of faith	May 1841		
140	Erastus H. Cook	Letter from church in Westminster, Vt	April 1869	Present member	
141	Mary M. Cook	"		"	
142	Minnie Cook	Profession of faith	Nov. 1849	"	
143	Elmore Cooper	"	July 1862	To church in Boston, Mass	Nov. 1867
144	Harriet H. Cooper	Letter from church in Alstead, N H	Oct. 1862		
145	Elizabeth Corbett	Profession of faith	May 1830	Non-resident before	
146	Samuel Crandall	"	Nov. 1821	Died in Westminster, Vt	Jan. 1840
147	Martha A. Crawford	"	Jan. 1899	Lives in Australia	Jan. 1853
148	Lucy J. (Foster) Cross	"	Nov. 1840	Present member	
149	Mehitable Cummings	Letter from church in Swanzey, N H	Feb. 1835	To 2d church, Keene	Oct. 1867
150	Maria H. Cummings	Letter from M E church, Keene, N H	Nov. 1869	Present member	

D.

No.	Name	Admission	Date	Status	Date
151	Sarah (Page) Dale	Letter from church in Roxbury, N H	May 1842	To church in Rutland, Mass	June 1892
152	Jane Damon	Letter from church in Fitzwilliam, N H	Sept. 1858	Died in Keene	Nov. 1872

3

No.	NAMES.	HOW ADMITTED.	DATE.	DISMISSIONS.	DATE.
133	Sukey Damon	Letter from church in Fitzwilliam, N H	Sept. 1866	Lives in Fitzwilliam, N H	Oct. 1852
134	Jabez W. Daniels	Member before	A.D. 1818	Died in Keene	June 1863
135	Eleanor Daniels	Profession of faith	Mar. 1832	Died in Rutland, Vt	Sept. 1834
136	Harriet Daniels	"	July 1858	To church in Rutland, Vt	
137	Harriet M. (Atherton) Darling	"	Sept. 1826	Lives in Chesterfield, N H	Oct. 1867
138	Daniel Darling	"	May 1832	To 2d church, Keene	
139	Theodosia (Stone) Darling	"	Oct. 1860	" "	Oct. 1863
160	Frances E. Darling	Letter from church in E Douglass, Mass	Mar. 1864	To church in Springfield, Mass	
161	Sarah L. Darling	Member before	A. D. 1818	Present member	
162	Anron Davis	Letter from church in Keene	Sept. 1882	Died in Keene	Mar. 1857
163	Mary Ann Davis	Letter from church in Worcester, Mass	1824	To church in Worcester, Mass	July 1858
164	Henry Day	Profession of faith	July 1868	Non-resident before	Jan. 1840
165	James C. Tay	"	July 1874	Present member	
166	Charlotte E. Day	Letter from church in Chester, Vt	Aug. 1841	Died in Keene	June 1876
167	Eliza Dean	Profession of faith	May 1857	Present member	
168	Laura C. Dean	"	1859	Died in Keene	
169	Sophia Dickinson	"	July 1876	Present member	Mar. 1861
170	Oren Dickinson	"	"	"	
171	Emily H. Dickinson	"	"	"	
172	Abbott W. Dickinson	"	"	"	
173	Addie E. Dickinson	"	"	"	
174	Herbert Dodge	Letter from church in Marlborough, N H	Nov. 1864	To church in Worcester, Mass	July 1869
175	Betsey Dorr	"	Mar. 1824	Non-resident before	Jan. 1840
176	Eli Dort	"	Jan. 1869	Present member	
177	Caroline E. Dort	Profession of faith	Mar. 1870	"	Mar. 1870
178	George G. Dort	"	"	"	
179	Eva J. Dort	"	Mar. 1876	To 2d church, Keene, N H	Oct. 1867
180	Mary E. Dort	"	Jan. 1861	"	
181	George P. Drown	"	May 1860	"	"
182	Elizabeth K. Drown	"	"	"	
183	Anna N. Duncan	Letter from church in Acworth, N H	Nov. 1866	Died in Keene	Apr. 1857
184	Mary J. Duncan	Profession of faith	Apr. 1840	To 2d church, Keene	Oct. 1867
185	Asa Duren	Letter from church in Concord, N H	Aug. 1823	Died in Keene	May 1854
186	Maria V. (Wood) Duren	"	Mar. 1864	To 2d church, Keene	Oct. 1867
187	Roxana W. Duren	Letter from church in Boston, Mass	1864	To 2d church, Keene	Sept. 1859
188	Ann W. Dwinnell	Profession of faith	July 1834	To church in Alstead, N H	

E.

No.	NAMES.	HOW ADMITTED.	DATE.	DISMISSIONS.	DATE.
189	Lucretia M. Elliot	Letter from church in Webster, Mass	Oct. 1872	Present member	Mar. 1860
190	Sarah P. (Thompson) Ellis	Profession of faith	Sept. 1857	To church in Swanzey, N H	

No.	Name	Manner of admission	Date	Status / Disposition	Date
191	Eugene S. Ellis	Profession of faith	Jan. 1882	Present member	April 1872
192	Elmina D. (Clark) Ellis	"	Sept. 1843	Died in Keene	
193	John Ellis	"	Nov. 1839	Present member	
194	Pamelia Ellis	Letter from church in Concord, Vt	July 1819	Present member	
195	Polly Ellis	Profession of faith	Sept. 1840	Died in Keene	July 1846
196	Hepsey Ellis	Letter from church in Harrisville, N H	Jan. 1853	"	Feb. 1873
197	Lucy (Wilson) Ellis	Profession of faith	Mar. 1823	"	Apr. 1871
198	Jacob Esty	"	Sept. 1826	"	Mar. 1890
199	Sophia Esty	"		To 2d church, Keene	Oct. 1867
200	Mary Esty	Letter from church in Sullivan N H	Nov. 1852	Died in Keene	Mar. 1858

F.

No.	Name	Manner of admission	Date	Status / Disposition	Date
201	Ebenezer Farnsworth	Member before	A.D. 1818	Non-resident before	Jan. 1840
202	J. Henry Farnsworth	Letter from church in Templeton, Mass	May 1866	To 2d church, Keene	Oct. 1867
203	Jane H. Farnsworth	Letter from church in Alstead, N H	April 1870	Present member	
204	Franklin Fay	"		"	
205	Jennie Fay	"		"	
206	Daniel Fisher	Member before	A.D. 1818	Died in Keene	Mar. 1859
207	Susan Fisher	Letter from church in Foxborough, Mass	Jan. 1828	"	Aug. 1864
208	Melia M. Fisher	Letter from church in Surry, N H	May 1853	To 2d church, Keene	Oct. 1867
209	Susan Fisher	Profession of faith	May 1859	"	
210	Kate F. (Spaulding) Flagg	"	Jun. 1869	To church in Townsend, Mass	June 1874
211	Frances A. (Shelley) Flint	"	Nov. 1883	Present member	
212	Ellen (Morse) Forbes	"	Sept. 1866	To church in Winchendon, Mass	Dec. 1869
213	Sarah H. Forbush	"	May 1872	Present member	
214	Stearns Foster	Letter from church in Stoddard, N H	Jan. 1869	"	
215	Mary Foster	Profession of faith	Jan. 1861	"	
216	Jennie F. Foster	Letter from church in Sullivan, N H	Mar. 1864	To 2d church, Keene	Oct. 1867
217	Jane S. Foster	Letter from church in Stoddard, N H	Nov. 1863	Present member	
218	Mary G. Foster	"	Jan. 1869	Present member	
219	Charles M. Foster	Profession of faith		"	
220	Warren Foster	"	Nov. 1863	To 2d church, Keene	Oct. 1867
221	Frank E. Foster	"	Mar. 1876	Present member	
222	Ruth A. Foster	"		"	
223	Herschel J. Fowler	Letter from church in Weymouth, Mass	May 1870	Lives in Chesterfield, N H	
224	Catharine M. Frazier	Profession of faith	Jan. 1866	To 2d church, Keene	Oct. 1867
225	Harriet E. Freeman	Profession of faith	July 1858	To Episcopal church, Keene	Sept. 1861
226	Lucy W. French	Letter from church in Westmoreland, N H	July 1835	Died in Keene	Dec. 1850
227	Hannah French	Profession of faith	May 1853	"	Jan. 1857
228	Esther French	"	July 1867	To 2d church, Keene	July 1867
229	Merlancy French	Letter from church in Peterboro', N H	Oct. 1851	To church in Peterboro', N H	Oct. 1858
230	Eliza French	Letter from church in Brattleboro', Vt	Jan. 1866	To 2d church, Keene	Oct. 1867

No.	NAMES	HOW ADMITTED	DATE	DISMISSIONS	DATE
251	Sarah French	Profession of faith	Jan. 1861	Died in Marlboro', N H	July 1865
252	Ellen G. French	"	May 1861	Died in Keene	Dec. 1866
253	Caroline E. French	"	Jan. 1864	To 2d church, Keene	Oct. 1867
254	Caroline L. French	Letter from church in Brattleboro', Vt	July 1866	Died in Keene	July 1867
255	Jotham A. French	Profession of faith	Oct. "	Died in Keene	Oct. 1867
256	Mary E. French	Letter from church in Milford, Mass	"	To 2d church, Keene	"
257	Polly Prink	Member before	"	"	
258	Loring C. Frost	Profession of faith	A. D. 1818	Died in Keene	Jan. 1854
259	Abigail Farber	"	May 1843	Died in Cleveland, O	Aug. 1863
			Nov. 1831	Died in Keene	July 1853
	G.				
240	Charles Gates	Letter from church in Antrim, N H	Feb. 1835	To church in Antrim, N H	Nov. 1856
241	Elizabeth Gates	Profession of faith	May 1840	Died in Logansport, Ind	
242	Elizabeth J. (Wilder) Gates	"	Mar. 1873	Present member	May 1856
243	Loretta (Morrison) Gebbes	"	Nov. 1831	"	
244	Samuel A. Gerould	"	Jan. 1836	Died in Keene	
245	Deborah D. Gerould	"	Jan. 1865	Present member	
246	Samuel A. Gerould, Jr	Letter from church in Wrentham, Mass	Sept. 1852	Lives in Worcester, Mass	
247	Susan F. Gerould	Profession of faith	July 1868	Died in Keene	
248	Fannie E. Gerould	"	Sept. 1844	To church in Concord, N H	Jan. 1852
249	Sybil (Mudell) Goole	"	Nov. 1865	Died in Keene	Dec. 1872
250	George Goodhue	Letter from church in Agawam, Mass	Oct. 1840	Died in Keene	Jan. 1858
251	Hepzibah Goodnow	Letter from church in Rutland, Mass	Nov. 1843	"	Mar. 1855
252	Charles E. Goodnow	Profession of faith	Sept. 1851	"	Jun. 1873
253	Sophia Goodnow	Letter from church in Stoddard, N H	Nov. 1843	"	May, 1875
254	Susan J. Gould	Profession of faith	April 1858	"	
255	Grace Ann Gould	"	Nov. 1876	Present member	
256	Cora Janette Gould	Letter from church in Leicester, Mass	July 1868	"	
257	Albert M. Goulding	Letter from church in Walpole, N H	May 1848	To church in Grafton, Mass	Oct. 1871
258	Amasa Graves	Profession of faith	Sept. 1843	Died in Keene	May 1866
259	Deborah Graves	"	May 1866	To 2d church, Keene	April 1803
260	Zebulon K. Graves	Letter from church in Alstead, N H	Dec. 1859	Died in Keene	Oct. 1867
261	Emily C. L. Graves	Profession of faith	May 1876	Present member	"
262	Silas R. Green	"	A. D. 1818	Died in Peoria, Ill	
263	Caroline L. Green	Member before	April 1845	To 2d church, Keene	Feb. 1870
264	Sophia (McCoy) Greenwood	Letter from church in Surry, N H	July 1863	Present member	Oct. 1867
265	Asa Griffin	"		Died in Peoria, Ill	"
266	Chloe Griffin	"		To 2d church, Keene	
267	Helen Maria Griffin	Profession of faith		Present member	

#	Name	Mode of admission	Date admitted	Disposition	Date
268	Francis H. Griffin	Profession of faith	July 1863	Died in Keene	June 1908
269	Susan A. (Willard) Griffin	"	Nov. 1868	"	July 1899
270	Roshun C. Griffith	Letter from church in Lowell, Mass	Jan. 1876	Present member	
271	Abigail Grimes	Profession of faith	Jan. 1828	Died in Keene	Sept. 1869
272	Thomas Grimes	"	May 1844	To 2d church, Keene	Oct. 1867
273	Nancy E. Grimes	"	Sept. 1857	"	"
274	Almira Grimes	"	July 1857	Present member	
275	John Grimes	Letter from church in Troy, N H	Nov. 1865	To 2d church, Keene	Oct. 1867
277	Julia A. Grimes	Profession of faith	Sept. 1836	"	
278	Lucinda Grimes	"	Sept. 1855	Present member	
279	Frances E. Grimes	"	Nov. 1831	"	
280	Mary D. Grimes	Letter from church in Springfield, Vt	Nov. 1876	"	
281	Marion F. Grinnell	Profession of faith	May 1841	Died in Keene	Oct. 1858
282	Thouns Gurler	Letter from church in Westmoreland, N H	Aug. 1841	Died in Milford, Mass	Mar. 1870
282	Abigail C. Gurler				

H.

#	Name	Mode of admission	Date admitted	Disposition	Date
283	William Hale	Letter from church in Hinsdale, N H	Nov. 1874	Died in Keene	May 1-76
284	Sebrana S. Hale	"	"	Present member	
285	Samuel W. Hale	Profession of faith	Jan. 1864	To 2d church, Keene	Oct. 1867
286	Emelia M. Hale	Letter from church in Dublin, N H	"	"	"
287	Julia Ann Hall	Profession of faith	Mar. 1832	Died in Keene	May 1856
288	Eliza McG. Hall	"	Nov. 1833	To church in Haydenville, Mass	Oct. 1865
289	Julia E. Hall	"	Mar. 1856	To Episcopal church, Keene	Nov. 1859
290	Samuel Ham	"	July 1876	Present member	
291	Diantha W. Ham				
292	Eliza A. Hamilton	Letter from church in Springfield, Ill	Apr. 1859	To church in Davenport, Iowa	Sept. 1865
293	Adaline R. Hamrock	Profession of faith	July 1850	Died in Keene	Sept. 1836
294	Julia (Pierce) Hardy	"	Mar. 1870		1875
295	Harriette L. (Utley) Harris	Letter from church in Bradford, N H	June 1842	To church in Westminster, Vt	Mar. 1855
296	Stewart Hastings	Letter from church in Boston, Mass	Oct. 1858	To church in Leavenworth, Kan	April 1861
297	Eliza P. (Withington) Hastings	Profession of faith	Mar. 1842	"	
298	Calvin Hastings	Letter from church in Marlboro', N H	Mar. 1874	Present member	
299	Eliza R. Hastings	Profession of faith		"	
300	Calvin W. Hastings	"	July 1876	"	
301	Fred. E. Hastings	"		"	
302	Ann E. (Hall) Hayden	"	Mar. 1843	To church in Haydenville, Mass	Oct. 1865
303	Isabel H. Hayes	"	Jan. 1864	To church in Brooklyn, N Y	Apr. 1870
304	Edward H. Hayward	Letter from church in Hancock, N H	Aug. 1869	Present member	
305	Emily Hayward	"		"	
306	Daniel K. Henley	Profession of faith	May 1871	"	
307	Emma R. Henley	"		"	

No.	Names.	How Admitted.	Date.	Dismissions.	Date.
308	Harriet Henton	Profession of faith	Mar. 1870	Present member	Sept. 1863
309	Nancy Heaton	Letter from church in Roxbury, N H	May 1840	Died in Keene	Oct. 1867
310	Asa C. Hemenway	Profession of faith	Jan. 1877	To 2d church, Keene	"
311	Harriet W. Hemenway	"	"	"	
312	Sophia E. Henry	Letter from church in Winchester, N H	May 1858		
313	Sarah D. Hills	Profession of faith	Jan. 1870	Present member	
314	Ellen M. Hills	"	July 1860	"	
315	Francis H. Hills	"	July 1861	"	
316	Cornelia I. Hirach	"	Mar. 1877	"	
317	Rufus C. Hitchcock	Letter from church in So Hadley Falls, Ms	June 1874	"	
318	Louise St. J. Hitchcock			"	
319	Daphne Hoar	Profession of faith	Sept. 1843	Died in Keene	Jan. 1873
320	Ambrose Hodgkins		Nov. 1858	Present member	
321	Lois L. W. Hodgkins	Letter from church in Townshend, Vt	July 1860	"	
322	Frances A. (Wilder) Holbrook	Profession of faith	Jan. 1856	Died in Keene	Nov. 1851
323	George E. Holbrook	"	July 1861	Present member	
324	Clara A. (French) Holbrook		May 1861	"	
325	Mary Holbrook	Letter from church in Athol, Mass	Oct. 1862	Died in Keene	May 1867
326	Sarah A. Holbrook	Letter from church in Hartford, Ct	May 1866	"	Nov. 1870
327	Mary A. Holbrook	Profession of faith	May 1900	Present member	
328	Leaha M. Holbrook	Letter from church in Linn, Ind	Sept. 1858	"	
329	George Holmes	Letter from church in Grafton, Vt	April 1847	"	
330	Lauretta C. Holmes			Died in Keene	July 1859
331	Mary L. Holmes	Letter from M E church, Keene	May 1861	Present member	April 1658
332	Sybil R. Holt	Letter from church in Nashua, N H	Nov. 1840	To church in Nelson, N H	
333	Joseph S. Holt	Profession of faith	July 1876	Present member	
334	Celestia M. Holt	"	Mar. 1864	"	
335	Frances M. Homer	"	July 1855	Died in Worcester, Mass	Jan. 1850
336	Sarah A. Howard	"	Nov. 1866	To 2d church, Keene	Oct. 1867
337	Betsey Howe	"	Nov. 1851	Present member	
338	Louisa Howe	"	"	To Baptist church, Peterboro', N H	
339	Abigail F. Howe	Letter from church in Gilsum, N H	May 1884	Died in Keene	Feb. 1851
340	Martin H. Howland	Profession of faith	Jan. 1870	Present member	Mar. 1873
341	Eliza A. Howland	"	April 1870	"	
342	Leonard C. Hubbard	Letter from church in Langdon, N H	May 1843	To church in Saxton's River, Vt	June 1881
343	Caroline P. Hubbard	"	"	"	
344	Sarah R. (Thompson) Hudson	Profession of faith	July 1866	To church in Gardner, Mass	Aug. 1868
345	Hiram Hudson	"	Sept. 1876	Died in Keene	Sept. 1876
346	Rosetta P. Hudson			Present member	

No.	Name	Mode of admission	Date	Remarks	Date
347	John Humphrey	Profession of faith	Jan. 1867	Present member	Jan. 1867
348	Eunice Humphrey	"	"	"	
349	Marietta Humphrey	"	July 1875	"	
350	Ellen M. (Ramd) Humphrey	"	Sept. 1853	To church in Waterbury, Vt	Jan. 1862
351	Alma C. L. Hunnewell	"	July 1876	Present member	
352	Philena Hurd	"	July 1851	To church in Sedgwick, Kan	Nov. 1874
353	Lydia Hurd	Letter from church in Chester, Vt	Dec. 1862	Lives in Athol, Mass	
354	Julia E. (Blake) Hurd	Profession of faith	May 1867	Present member	Aug. 1857
355	Eliza A. (Dean) Hutchins	"	July 1851	To church in Melrose, Mass	Feb. 1856
356	Mary J. (Darling) Hutchins	"	Mar. 1849	To church in Winchester, N H	Oct. 1867
357	Lucy L. Hutchins	Letter from church in Putney, Vt	Nov. 1858	To 2d church, Keene	Oct. 1867
358	Lydia L. Hutchins	Letter from church in Troy, N H	Jan. 1845	To church in Bowen's Prairie, Iowa	Nov. 1866
359	Martha S. Hutchins	Profession of faith	May 1861	"	
360	Charles W. Hyde	Letter from church in Gilead, Conn	Mar. 1874	Present member	
361	Frances M. G. Hyde	Profession of faith	July 1876	"	
362	Julia F. Hyland	Letter from church in Stoddard, N H	Sept. 1858	To 2d church, Keene, N H	Oct. 1867
	I.				
363	Horace N. Irish	Profession of faith	Jan. 1869	Present member	Aug. 1853
364	Eliza E. (Port) Irish	"	Sept. 1866	"	Oct. 1875
365	Gardner W. Isham	"	Jan. 1875	"	June 1875
366	Sarah J. Isham	"	"	"	Oct. 1867
	J.				
367	Phebe S. (Fowler) Jameson	Profession of faith	Nov. 1831	Died in Keene	Nov. 1831
368	Mary (Woodward) Johnson	"	Sept. 1835	"	
369	Paulina Johnson	Letter from M E church, Keene	June 1865	To 2d church, Keene	Oct. 1867
370	Sophia (Arnold) Johnson	Profession of faith	Nov. 1858	To church in Westminster, Vt	June 1875
371	John E. Jones	Letter from church in Fitchburg, Mass	May 1826	To 2d church, Keene	Oct. 1875
372	Martha L. Jones	Profession of faith	July 1876	Present member	
373	Robert C. Jones	"	"	"	
374	Mary A. H. Jones	"	Jan. 1853	To church in Worcester, Mass	April 1858
375	Isaac R. Joslin	"	Mar. 1856	Died in Keene	June 1875
376	Luke Joslin	Letter from church in Stoddard, N H	Jan. 1852	Present member	
377	Lydia F. Joslin	Profession of faith	Jan. 1852	"	
378	Susan A. (Wilson) Joslin	"	Nov. 1856	"	
379	Sarah R. Joslin	"	Nov. 1839	"	
380	Sarah H. Joslin	"		"	
381	Merry Joy	Member before	A.D. 1818	Non-resident before	Jan. 1840
	K.				
382	Lucasta N. Karr	Letter from church in Brooklyn, N Y	Jan. 1869	To church in Cambridgeport, Mass	Jan. 1873
383	Mary L. Karr	Profession of faith	Nov. 1860	"	Nov. 1860
384	John E. Kellogg	"	Jan. 1853	To church in Norwich, Conn	Apr. 1859
385	Ezra O. Kemp	"	May 1895	To 2d church, Keene	Oct. 1897

No.	Names	How Admitted	Date	Dismissions	Date
386	Maria A. Kemp	Profession of faith	May 1862	To 2d church, Keene	Oct. 1867
387	Thomas M. Kenney	"	May 1871	Present member	
388	Sybil Keyes	Member before	A.D. 1818	Died in Keene	Mar. 1851
389	Charles Keyes	Profession of faith	Nov. 1836	Died in Keene	May 1874
390	Elizabeth E. Keyes	Letter from church in Rochester, Vt	May 1844	Present member	
391	Clara I. Keyes	Profession of faith	Jan. 1870	"	
392	Mary E. Kiblin	"	July 1863	Died in Keene	Jan. 1864
393	Arba Kidder	"	Mar. 1832	Present member	
394	Mary E. Kidder	"	Sept. 1831	"	
395	Esther Kilburn	Letter from church in Walpole, N H	May 1863	To 2d church, Keene	
396	Elizabeth (Woodward) King	Profession of faith	Mar. 1837	To church in Olivet, Mich	Nov. 1867
397	Lucinda R. Kingman	Letter from M. E. church, Keene	June 1865	Present member	
398	Sarah E. Kingman	Profession of faith	July 1864	"	
399	Abijah Kingsbury	Member before	A.D. 1818	Died in Keene	Oct. 1854
400	Abigail W. Kingsbury	Profession of faith	Nov. 1831	To Episcopal church, Keene	Oct. 1860
401	Betsy Kingsbury	"	May 1843	Died in Keene	Nov. 1866
402	Delilah H. Kingsbury	"		Died in Keene	April 1866
403	Albert Kingsbury	"		Died in Keene	Dec. 1870
404	Ann E. Kingsbury	"		Present member	
405	George Kingsbury	"	Sept. 1843	To 2d church, Keene	Oct. 1867
406	Lydia W. Kingsbury	"	July 1843	"	"
407	Ella A. Kingsbury	"	Mar. 1870	Died in Peterboro', N H	July 1874
408	Mary H. Kingsbury	"	May 1853	Present member	
409	Susan E. (Brooks) Knight	"	Sept. 1853	To 2d church, Keene	Oct. 1867
	L.				
410	Margaret Lamson	Member before	A.D. 1818	Died in Keene	Jan. 1861
411	William Lamson	Profession of faith	Mar. 1834	Died in Keene	Jan. 1860
412	Elisha F. Lane	Letter from church in Marlboro', N H	Oct. 1872	Present member	
413	Harriet P. (Wilder) Lane	Profession of faith		Present member	
414	Rachel I. Lane	Letter from church in Swanzey, N H	Oct. 1863	Present member	
415	Hannah Lawrence	Letter from church in Roxbury, N H	July 1864	Died in Keene	May 1867
416	Stella E. Leach	Letter from church in Townshend, Vt	Jan. 1867	To 2d church, Keene	Oct. 1867
417	Patty Leland	Profession of faith	Nov. 1836	Present member	
418	Martha A. Leonard	Letter from M. E. church, Lowell, Mass	Jan. 1876	"	
419	Abby B. Leverett	Profession of faith	Jan. 1844	"	
420	Kate F. Leverett	"	May 1861	"	
421	Frank J. Leverett	"	July 1861	Died in the Army	Oct. 1863
422	Ezra Livermore	Letter from church in Alstead, N H	Jan. 1855	To 2d church, Keene	Oct. 1867
423	Betsey Livermore	"		"	"

	Name	Mode of admission	Date admitted	Disposition	Date
424	Henrietta V. Loveland	Letter from church in Norwich, Conn	Mar. 1869	Present member	
425	Ellen M. (Hartwell) Lovell	Letter from church in Troy, N Y	July 1868	To church in Chatfield, Minn	Mar. 1870
426	Rosina W. Lyman	Profession of faith	Jan. 1869	Present member	
427	Anna K. (Maynard) Lyman	"	July 1866	"	
428	Lizzie G. Lyman	"	July 1871	"	
429	Elizabeth T. (Gray) Lyman	Letter from church in Templeton, Mass	Sept. 1868	"	
	M.				
430	Catherine Mann	Profession of faith	May 1860	Non-resident member	
431	James H. Mark	"	Sept. 1867	To 2d church, Keene	Oct. 1867
432	Chloe Marsh	"	Nov. 1831	Died in Keene	Apr. 1861
433	Candace Marsh	"	Dec. 1870	Present member	
434	Walter E. Marsh	"	July 1876	"	
435	Ella Marshall	"	Mar. 1873	"	
436	Eloisa (Shelley) Mason	Letter from church in Orange, Mass	Sept. 1852	To church in Sullivan, N H	June 1857
437	Asa Maynard	"	Sept. 1864	Died in Keene	Sept. 1872
438	Rhoda Maynard	Profession of faith		Present member	
439	Jennie M. McAllister	"	May 1871	"	
440	George W. McDuffee	"	May 1906	To 2d church, Keene	Oct. 1867
441	Ellen M. McDuffee	"		"	
442	Samuel V. McDuffee	Letter from church in Amherst Coll, Mass	June 1866	"	May 1868
443	Mary L. W. McLane	Profession of faith	July 1826	Present member	
444	Rebecca Metcalf	Member before	A. D. 1818	Died in Keene	May 1851
445	Hepzebah Metcalf	"	Mar.	Died in Roxbury, N H	
446	Edwin G. Metcalf	Profession of faith	1824	Present member	
447	Martha S. Metcalf	Letter from church in Boston, Mass	Nov. 1852	"	
448	William Metcalf	Profession of faith	July 1831	"	
449	Amanda Metcalf	"	Nov. 1831	"	
450	Alvah E. Metcalf	"	Mar. 1832	"	
451	Harriet M. Metcalf	Letter from church in Alstead, N H	Jan. 1853	"	
452	Thankful Metcalf	Profession of faith	Nov. 1840	"	
453	Almira R. Metcalf	"	Jan. 1849	To 2d church, Keene	Oct. 1867
454	William F. Metcalf	"	May 1861	Died in Chelsea, Mass	Aug. 1872
455	Sarah E. Metcalf	"	Jan. 1868	Present member	
456	Charles F. Millikin	Letter from church in Littleton, N H	Mar. 1851	To church in Littleton, N H	Sept. 1860
457	Betsey Morrison	Profession of faith	Oct. 1860	Present member	
458	Julia A. Morrison	"	Nov. 1869	"	
459	Sarah Morrison	"	Mar. 1873	"	
460	Elizabeth (Toole) Morse	Letter from church in Northfield, Mass	May 1854	Died in Keene	Sept. 1869
461	Lydia Muchmoro	"	Apr. 1847	To 2d church, Keene	Oct. 1867
	N.				
462	Hannah Newcomb	Member before	A. D. 1818	Died in Keene	Sept. 1831
463	Sarah Newcomb	Letter from church in Westmoreland, N H	Nov. 1835	Died in Keene	June 1873

No.	NAMES.	HOW ADMITTED.	DATE.	DISMISSIONS.	DATE.
464	Hannah D. Newcomb	Profession of faith	Sept. 1852	To church in Walpole, N H	Aug. 1857
465	Rebecca Newell	"	May 1858	Present member	April 1868
466	Mary A. (Metcalf) Newell	"	May 1461	To church in Chelsea, Mass	April 1855
467	Roswell Nims	"	Sept. 1852	Died in Keene	Oct. 1857
468	Sally Nims	Member before	A. D. 1818		
469	Emily M. Nims	Profession of faith	Nov. 1853	Non-resident member	
470	Lydia L. Nims	Letter from church in Sullivan, N H	May 1846	Died in Keene	Feb. 1851
471	Mary R. Nims	Profession of faith	Dec. 1862	To 2d church, Keene	Oct. 1867
472	Albert G. Nims	"	Nov. 1855	"	"
473	Harriette A. (Thompson) Nims				
474	Granville W. Nims	"	Nov. 1866	"	Mar. 1868
475	Mary A. Nims	"	July 1865	"	Oct. 1867
476	Ainsworth M. Nims	"	Mar. 1876	Present member	
477	George H. Nims	Letter from church in Sullivan, N H	May 1871	"	
478	Ruth A. Nims	"		"	
479	Francis O. Nims	"		"	
480	Ella L. Nims	Profession of faith	May 1871	"	
481	Lewis C. Noble	Letter from church in Chaplin, Conn	Jan. 1870	"	
482	Sibyl Norton	Letter from church in Brooklin, Vt	Nov. 1881	Died in Keene	
483	Anna Nurse	Letter from church in Littleton, Mass	May 1822	"	
484	Apollos Nye	Profession of faith	Nov. 1835	"	
485	Lucy K. Nye	"	July 1835	"	
486	Fanny C. Nye	Letter from church in Swanzey, N H	Feb. 1835	To 2d church, Keene	
	O.				
487	William Olcott	Profession of faith	May 1871	Died in Keene	Feb. 1876
488	Mary Olcott	Letter from church in Peterboro', N H	Jan. 1845	Present member	
489	Stephen D. Osborne	Profession of faith	Sept. 1858	To 2d church, Keene	Oct. 1867
490	Maria R. Osborne	"		"	"
491	Jonah Osgood	Member before	A. D. 1816	Died in Keene	June 1853
492	George Osgood	Profession of faith	May 1843	Lives in California	
493	Philinda Osgood	"	Sept. 1843	Died in Keene	Sept. 1874
494	Maria R. Osgood	"	Jan. 1851	Died in Chicago, Ill	Sept. 1855
	P.				
495	Silas Page	Profession of faith	Nov. 1836	Present member	
496	Lydia H. Page	Letter from church in Gilsum, N H	May 1842	"	
497	Rebecca T. Page	Letter from church in Bridgewater, Mass	Aug. 1826	Died in Keene	May 1864
498	Betsey Parker	Member before	A. D. 1818	"	Aug. 1865
499	Prudence Parker	"	"	To church in Newton Corners, Mass	Oct. 1865
500	Jotham Parker	Profession of faith	July 1843	Died in Keene	Mar. 1866

No.	Name	Admission	Date	Status	Date
501	Polly Parker	Letter from church in Roxbury, N H	Jan. 1844	Died in Keene	Feb. 1865
502	Jemine O. Parker	Letter from church in Boonville, Mo	Aug. 1850	To church in South Boston, Mass	April 1866
503	Sally H. Parker	Profession of faith	Nov. 1888	Died in Keene	Nov. 1875
504	Henry E. Parker	"	May 1896	To church in Hanover, N H	Mar. 1866
505	Elizabeth E. Parker	"	Sept. 1832	Lives in New York City	
506	Julia A. H. Parker	"	Nov. 1862	"	
507	Mary (Kingsbury) Parker	"	May 1843	Present member	
508	Mary A. Parker	"	Mar. 1868	Died in Keene	July 1870
509	Dolly Ann Patterson	Letter from church in Nashua, N H	Mar. 1865	Lives in Nashua, N H	
510	Harvey F. Patterson	Profession of faith	May 1870	Present member	
511	Helen M. Patterson	"	May 1871	"	
512	Martha F. Perry	Letter from church in Pittsfield, Mass	May 1848	Died in Keene	July 1857
513	Benjamin F. Phelps	Letter from church in Alstead, N H	Jan. 1856	To church in Ashburnham, Mass	Dec. 1868
514	Emeline F. Phelps	"	"	"	"
515	Polly Phelps				
516	Lois W. Phelps				
517	Jonas Phelps	Letter from church in Templeton, Mass	May 1861	Died in Keene	May 1876
518	Abigail Phelps	"	"	Present member	Oct. 1875
519	Sarah E. Phelps	Profession of faith	Dec. 1871	To church in Templeton, Mass	
520	Harvey Phillips	Profession of faith in Harrisville, N H	May 1870	Lives in Templeton, Mass	
521	Elvira Phillips	Profession of faith	May 1871	Present member	
522	Gardner Phillips	Letter from church in Walpole, N H	Aug. 1841	Died in Keene	Dec. 1869
523	Pamelia C. Phillips	Letter from church in Westminster, Vt	"	Lives in Westminster, Vt	
524	Frances M. Phillips	Profession of faith	July 1895	To 2d church, Keene	Oct. 1877
525	Sophia C. Pierce	"	Sept. 1884	Present member	
526	Mary J. (Reed) Pierce	"	Sept. 1862	To church in Pekin, Ill.	Mar. 1868
527	Sophronia E. Pond	"	Mar. 1876	Present member	
528	Elvira F. (Wilder) Poole	"	Sept. 1843	"	
529	Ellen E. (Dickinson) Porter	Letter from church in Winchester, N H	Nov. 1859	"	
530	Emily M. (Wheaton) Porter	Profession of faith	Jan. 1870	Died in Keene	Mar. 1871
531	Maria M. Porter	"	May 1882	Died in Keene	Oct. 1864
532	Alice G. Porter	"	Mar. 1870	Present member	
533	Mary (Cook) Pratt	"	Jan. 1844	Died in Keene	Aug. 1851
534	Charlotte N. Pray	Letter from church in Lebanon, N H	Sept. 1843	Present member	
535	Mary A. (Marsh) Preckle	Profession of faith	Sept. 1843	To M. E. church, Keene	Nov. 1851
536	Catharine Presler	"	May 1862	To 2d church, Keene	Oct. 1857
537	John F. Prindell	"	May 1875	To M. E. church, Keene	Sept. 1857
538	Miranda E. Prindell	"	May 1880	"	
539	Jane E. Proctor	Letter from Bap. church in Malone, N Y	May 1840	Present member	
540	Charles G. Putney	Letter from church in Henniker, N H	Jan. 1869	To church in Orange, Mass	Dec. 1871
541	Izora M. Putney	Profession of faith	Sept. 1870	"	"

No	NAMES	HOW ADMITTED	DATE	DISMISSIONS	DATE
	R.				
542	Laura E. (Dunbar) Ralston	Profession of faith	Mar. 1832	Joined Episcopal ch., Lockport, N Y	July 1859
543	Anna Rand	Member before	A.D. 1818	Died in Keene	
544	Elisha Rand	Letter from church in Alstead, N H	May 1817	To 2d church, Keene	Oct. 1865
545	Lydia (Griffin) Rand	Letter from church in Acworth, N H	Feb. 1851	Died in Keene	Sept. 1855
546	Frances M. (Sturtevant) Rand	Profession of faith	Jan. 1863	To 2d church, Keene	Oct. 1887
547	George H. Rand	"	May 1843	Died in Brooklyn, N Y	Oct. 1874
548	Isaac Rand	"	Sept. 1830	To 2d church, Keene	Oct. 1887
549	Julia A. (Kingsbury) Rand	"	Jan. 1852	"	"
550	Lyman F. Rand	"	Sept. 1861		
551	Deborah D. (Gerould) Ranney	"	Mar. 1843	Present member	
552	Charlotte K. (Fletcher) Lawson	"	Sept. 1856	To church in Amherst, Mass	Feb. 1870
553	Joel Reed	Letter from church in Swanzey, N H	Feb. 1866	Present member	
554	Helen M. Reed	"		Present member	
555	Mary Reed	Profession of faith	Sept. 1826	To M. E. church, Keene	
556	Susan Rest	"	Mar. 1876	Present member	
557	Melinda F. Rhodes	Letter from church in Brattleboro', Vt	Dec. 1862	Lives in Brattleboro', Vt	
558	Juliette A. (Hall) Rhodes	Profession of faith	Jan. 1864	Lives in Boston, Mass	
559	Elvira Richardson	Letter from church in Rochester, Vt	Oct. 1860	Present member	
560	Lauretta P. Richardson	Profession of faith	Mar. 1870	To church in Hilo, Sandwich Islands	Sept. 1871
561	Sarah M. (Goodnow) Richartison	"	Jan. 1853	To 2d church, Keene	Oct. 1887
562	Rev. Cyrus Richarleson	Letter from church in Dracut, Mass	Mar. 1877	Present member	
563	Anna D. Richarlson	Letter from church in Plymouth, N H	Oct. 1874	"	
564	Clara H. Richards	Profession of faith	May 1874	"	
565	Harriet Ripley	Letter from church in Troy, N H	Dec. 1875	"	
566	Mary C. Ripley	"		"	
567	Franklin Ripley	"		"	
568	Mary R. Ripley	"		"	
569	Harriet R. Ripley	"		"	
570	Martha B. Ripley	Profession of faith	Jan. 1876	"	
571	George Rising	Letter from church in Suffield, Conn	May 1842	To church in Kansas Ter	Sept. 1855
572	Sarah (Kingsbury) Rising	Profession of faith	Sept. 1827	"	
573	Clara E. (Moore) Robinson	"	Mar. 1870	Present member	
574	George W. Rollins	Letter from church in Boston, Mass	Sept. 1847	Non-resident member	
575	Abby Ann Rollins	"		"	
576	Sarah Rugg	Profession of faith	May 1819	Died in Keene	Jan. 1854
577	Frank A. Rugg	"	July 1876	Present member	
578	Henrietta Ruffle	"	July 1864	To 2d church, Keene	Oct. 1867
579	Harriet Ruffle	"	Mar. 1865	To church in Stoddard, N H	Mar. 1866

No.	Name	Admission	Date admitted	Status	Date removed
580	Charles Russell	Letter from Baptist church, Dublin, N H	Jan. 1862	To church in Rochester, N Y	Feb. 1866
581	Olivo Russell	Letter from church in Winchester, N H	July "	"	"
582	Delia I. T. Russell	Profession of faith	July 1876	Present member	:
583	Flora E. Sargent	Profession of faith	July 1875	Present member	:
584	Joel Saunders	Letter from church in Fitzwilliam, N H	Dec. 1836	Died in Keene	Mar. 1870
585	Mary Saunders	Letter from church in Concord, N H	Nov. 1836	Present member	:
586	Albert H. Sawtelle	Profession of faith	May "	Lives in Fitchburg, Mass	:
587	Abbie A. Sawtelle	"		Died in Keene	Dec. 1870
588	Tristram Sawyer	Letter from church in Nashua, N H	Nov. 1866	To 2d church, Keene	Oct. 1867
589	Sarah J. Sawyer	"	"	"	
590	Jane Sawyer	Profession of faith	Nov. 1836	Died in Keene	Dec. 1863
591	Andrew C. Sears	"	July "	Present member	
592	Julia A. Sears	"	"	"	
593	Persis R. (Kingman) Shaw	"	July 1864	To church in Bridgewater, Mass	Oct. 1868
594	Frances A. (Pond) Shelton	"	May 1858	Present member	
595	Roana Shelley	Letter from church in Surry, N H	July 1846	"	
596	Lucy A. Shelley	Profession of faith	Nov. 1862	To 2d church, Keene	Dec. 1870
597	Ida M. Sherman	"	Jan. 1877	Present member	
598	Lucy Shurtleff	Letter from church in Lancaster, Mass	Dec. 1846	Non-resident before	Jan. 1840
599	David B. Silsby	Profession of faith		Non-resident before	
600	Frances M. (French) Silsby	"	Mar. 1865	To 2d church, Keene	Oct. 1897
601	Hannah M. Simonds				Nov. 1869
602	Betsey Skinner	Letter from church in Chesterfield, N H	Nov. 1868	Died in Keene	Nov. 1869
603	Azro R. Skinner	Profession of faith	June 1866	Present member	
604	Sophie C. Skinner	Letter from church in Hinsdale, N H	July 1868	"	
605	Dudley Smith	Profession of faith	Sept. 1840	To church in De Kalb, Ill	Aug. 1857
606	Betsey G. Smith	Letter from church in Concord, N H	Jan. 1840	"	"
607	Sarah H. (Grimes) Smith	Profession of faith	Jan. 1832	"	"
608	Sarah Smith	"	Nov. 1825	Died in Keene	July 1859
609	Mary A. (Emerson) Smith	"	May 1834	To church in Gilsum, N H	Nov. 1851
610	Henry L. Smith	"	Sept. 1864	To 2d church, Keene	Apr. 1851
611	Elizabeth M. (Foster) Smith	"	July 1863	"	Oct. 1887
612	Esther (Thompson) Smith	"	July 1868	Non-resident member	
613	Mary S. (Dickinson) Smith	"	Nov. 1839	To church in St. Louis, Mo	Nov. 1858
614	Sally Smith	"	A. D. 1818	Died in Keene	June 1858
615	Sally (Sturtevant) Snow	Member before		"	May 1856
616	Sylvia Snow	Letter from Baptist church, Keene	July 1844	To 2d church, Keene	Oct. 1867
617	Martha A. H. Spalter	Letter from church in Westford, Mass	Sept. 1856	Present member	
618	Adelle C. Spalter	Profession of faith	July 1870	"	
619	Mary G. Spalter	"	July 1871	"	
620	Wilton H. Spalter	"	May 1871	"	

No.	NAMES.	HOW ADMITTED.	DATE.	DISMISSIONS.	DATE
621	Emma A. (Marsh) Spalter	Profession of faith	Mar. 1870	Present member	
622	Erastus Spaulding	Letter from church in Troy, N H	Jan. 1856	To 2d church, Keene	Oct. 1857
623	Mary E. Spaulding	"	"	"	"
624	Henry O. Spaulding	Letter from church in Sullivan, N H	Jan. 1864	"	"
625	Susan H. Spaulding	"	"	"	
626	Lucy P. Spaulding	Profession of faith	Nov. 1858		
627	Lisette W. (Morrison) Spaulding	"	Nov. 186?	Present member	
628	Lois S. Spear	"	Jan. 1865	"	
629	Solon W. Stone	Letter from church in Marlboro', N H	Dec. 1875	"	
630	Maria L. Stone	"	Jan. 1876	Died in Keene	Apr. 1876
631	Gertrude E. Stone	Profession of faith	Nov. 1876	Present member	
632	Charles Wm. Stone	Member before	A. D. 1818	Non-resident before	
633	Militiah Strong	Profession of faith	Nov. 1852	Died in Keene	Jan. 1840
634	Luther Sturtevant	"	Nov. 1825	"	Dec. 1863
635	Sarah Sturtevant	"	Mar. 1826	Present member	May 1853
636	Lindamira Sturtevant	Letter from church in Wethersfield, Vt.	Feb. 1838	"	
637	Isabella L. Sturtevant	Profession of faith	May 1862	"	
638	Ellen M. Sturtevant	Letter from church in Ludlow, Vt	Oct. 1856	To church in Framingham, Mass.	Jan. 1859
639	William Symmes			"	
640	Eliza A. Symmes				
641	Caroline R. Symonds	Letter from church in Sullivan, N H	July 1876	Present member	

T.

No.	NAMES.	HOW ADMITTED.	DATE.	DISMISSIONS.	DATE
642	Martha B. (Wilder) Taft	Profession of faith	May 1840	To church in Worcester, Mass	Dec. 1855
643	Nancy R. Taft	Letter from church in Nelson, N H	Sept. 1867	To 2d church, Keene	Oct. 1867
644	Marietta N. Taft	Profession of faith	Sept. 1859	"	
645	Emoretta M. Taft	"	May 190?	Died in Nashua, N H.	Dec. 1873
646	Mary S. (Blake) Tardox	"	Sept. 1847	To church in Wapello, Iowa	April 1863
647	Augusta H. (Leverett) Taylor	Member before	A. D. 1818	To church in Boston, Mass	Sept. 1864
648	Fanny Fletcher	"		Died in Keene	June 1857
649	Sally Thayer	Profession of faith	Mar. 1855	To 2d church, Keene	Oct. 1867
650	Harriet C. Thomas	Letter from church in Sullivan, N H	Dec. 1824	Died in Keene	July 1857
651	Betsey Thompson	Profession of faith	Sept. 1857	To church in Swampscott, Mass	Oct. 1869
652	Maria (Burgess) Thompson	"	Nov. 1859	Lives in Springfield, Mass	
653	Benjamin F. Thompson	"	Jan. 1861	"	
654	Carrie (Everett) Thompson	"	Jan. 1824	Present member	
655	Sally Thompson	Letter from church in Danvers, Mass	July 1866	"	
656	Emma J. Thompson	Profession of faith		Present member	
657	Sarah Relief Thompson	"		To church in Gardner, Mass	Aug. 1868
658	Cynthia L. Tilden	"	Jan. 1862	Present member	

No.	Name	Mode of admission	Date	Status	Date
659	Laura R. Tilden	Profession of faith	Mar. 1870	Present member	
660	Kate L. Tilden	"		"	
661	Sarah Tolman		May 1843	Non-resident member	
662	J C. Tolman	Letter from church in Hinsdale, N H	May 1866	To church in Bellows Falls, Vt	Dec. 1867
663	A. F. Tolman	"		"	
664	Lucella Tolman	Profession of faith	July 1866	"	
665	Mary M. (Keed) Tolman	"	Sept. 1837	To church in Marlborough, N H	April 1862
666	William Torrance	Letter from church in Ann Arbor, Mich	Nov. 1852	Died in Keene	Feb. 1855
667	Elizabeth Totten	Profession of faith	Nov. 1856	To church in Leominster, Mass	Oct. 1861
668	Andrew D. Towne	Letter from church in Gilsum, N H	June 1865	To 2d church, Keene	Oct. 1867
669	Eliza A. Towne	Profession of faith	July 1866		
670	Sarah E. Towne	Letter from church in Marlow, N H	June 1865	Died in Keene	July 1865
671	Andrew Towne	Letter from church in Gilsum, N H	1869	"	Aug. 1870
672	Sally Towne	Profession of faith	May 1871	"	July 1869
673	Lizzie M. Towne	Letter from church in Alstead, N H	Nov. 1851		
674	Harriet W. Towne	Profession of faith	Dec. 1862	Present member	
675	Mary W. Towns	Letter from church in Troy, N H	May 1871	To 2d church, Keene	Oct. 1867
676	Laura M. Townshend	Profession of faith		Present member	
677	Leonard J. Tuttle	"	Sept. 1851		
678	Susan M. Tuttle				
679	Marian R. (Willson) Twiss		June 1858	To church in Holyoke, Mass	Oct. 1853
	U.				
680	Georgiana A. (Henderson) Upham	Letter from church in Newport, N H	Nov. 1863	Non-resident member	
	W.				
681	Mary (Carpenter) Wallace	Profession of faith	Sept. 1852	To church in Hoosick Falls, N Y	July 1867
682	Jerusha E. Wallace	"	May 1871	Lives in Weymouth, Mass	
683	Leonard Wellington	"	Aug. 1870	Present member	
684	Hattie I. Wellington	Letter from Bap. church, Woodstock, Conn	May 1871		
685	Jerry P. Wellman	Profession of faith			
686	Lucy A. Wellman	"	Nov. 1841		
687	Mary (Metcalf) Wells	Member before	A. D. 1818	Non-resident member	Oct. 1861
688	Lydia Wetherbee	Letter from church in Gilsum, N H	May 1841	Died in Boston, Mass	
689	Esther R. Wetherbee	Letter from church in Winchester, N H	Jan. 1870	To church in Wethersfield, Vt	June 1850
690	Abbie T. Wheaton	Profession of faith	July 1840	Lives in Winchester, N H	
691	Mary A. Wheeler	"	May 1854	To 2d church, Keene	Oct. 1847
692	John Q. Wheeler	"	Sept. 1854	To 2d church, Keene	Mar. 1864
693	Helen M. Wheeler	"	Mar. 1856		Aug. 1853
694	Martha A. Wheeler	"	July 1866	Died in Keene	Oct. 1867
695	Joseph P. Whitcomb	Letter from church in Swanzey, N H	Dec. 1862	To 2d church, Keene	
696	Mary E. (Goodnow) Whitcomb	Member before	A. D. 1818	Non-resident before	
697	Mary White	"	April 1858	Non-resident before	Jan. 1840
698	Major White	Letter from church in Winchester, N H		To 2d church, Keene	Oct. 1897

No.	Names	How Admitted	Date	Dismissions	Date
699	Eunice (Chase) White	Letter from church in Winchester, N H	April 1858	To 2d church, Keene	Oct. 1867
700	Shubael White	Profession of faith	Nov. 1871	Present member	
701	Nancy L. White	Letter from church in Boston, Mass	Nov. 1841	"	
702	William H. White	Profession of faith	Nov. 1859	To Park street church, Boston, Mass	Mar. 1859
703	Frederic A. White	Profession of faith	July 1876	Present member	
704	George Whitney	Letter from church in Nelson, N H	May 1867	To 2d church, Keene	Oct. 1867
705	Nancy Whitney	"		"	"
706	Eugene M. Whitney	Profession of faith	July 1866	"	
707	Thomas H. Whitney	"	Sept. 1867	"	
708	Charles H. Whitney	Letter from church in Nelson, N H	Dec. 1874	Present member	
709	Lucy C. Whitney	"		"	
710	Charles R. Whitney	"		"	
711	Mattie (Page) Whitney	"		Died in Keene	
712	Martha Wilder	Profession of faith	A. D. 1816	"	Jan. 1875
713	Silas Wilder	Member before	Sept. 1819	To church in Herkimer, N Y	Jan. 1801
714	Lydia J. Wilder	Profession of faith	Jan. 1820	Died in Chester, Vt	Dec. 1872
715	Rhoda J. Wilder	"	Sept. 1827	Died in Keene	April 1895
716	Rhoda Jane Wilder	"	Nov. 1853	To 2d church, Keene	April 1871
717	Axel Wilder	"	Sept. 1843	Died in Keene	Oct. 1867
718	Elvira W. Wilder	"		"	April 1860
719	Susan M. Wilder	"	Jan. 1859	"	Jan. 1863
720	Solon S. Wilkinson	Letter from church in Marlboro', N H		Present member	
721	Chestina B. Wilkinson	Profession of faith	July 1876	"	
722	Edward H. Wilkinson	"	Nov. 1821	Died in Keene	
723	Lockhart Willard	"	May 1822	"	Jan. 1867
724	Sally (Nurse) Willard	"	May 1866	Present member	July 1868
725	William Willard	"	Nov. 1841	"	
726	Lucretia Willard	"	Nov. 1831	"	
727	Sally (Howe) Willard	"	May 1851	To church in Troy, N H	Oct. 1858
728	Irene F. (Nye) Willard	"	May 1862	Present member	
729	Aurelia (Thompson) Willard	"	July 1869	"	
730	Lucy R. Willard	"	Jan. 1870	"	
731	Katie J. Willard	"	Sept. 1840	To church in Providence, R I	Mar. 1852
732	Martin (Wheeler) Williams	"	Jan. 1852	Present member	
733	Jehiel Willson	Letter from church in Harrisville, N H	Jan. 1853	"	
734	Lucy C. Willson	Profession of faith	Jan. 1853	"	
735	Mary E. Willson	"	July 1851	"	
736	Helen E. Willson	"	Jan. 1853	"	
737	Eliza Willson	"	July 1852		

No.	Name	Admitted by	Date	Disposition	Date
738	Gardiner Wilson		Oct. 1839	Died in Keene	Mar. 1852
739	Martha A. Wilson	Letter from church in Acworth, N H	May 1871	To church in Westboro', Mass	Mar. "
740	William O. Wilson	Letter from church in Westboro', Mass		Present member	
741	Harriet M. Wilson	Profession of faith	July 1866	Died in Keene	Mar. 1877
742	Abbie M. Wilson	Letter from church in Sullivan, N H	Jan. 1836	"	Mar. 1859
743	Nancy C. Wilson	Profession of faith	Sept. 1828	"	Aug. 1858
744	Abigail D. (Metcalf) Willson		July 1834	To church in Roxbury, N H	June 1855
745	Mary Wilson	Letter from church in Roxbury, N H	Sept. 1845	To church in Grand Rapids, Mich	Sept. 1854
746	Enoch W. Winchester	Profession of faith	May 1839	"	
747	A. Martha (Kingsbury) Winchester	"	Dec. 1853	Died in Keene	Dec. 1861
748	Nathan Wood	Letter from church in Walpole, N H		"	June 1867
749	Maria T. Wood		May 1855	Present member	
750	Sarah L. Wood	Profession of faith	Nov. 1862	Lives in New York City	
751	Mary M. (Parker) Wood	"	Apr. 1870	Present member	May 1866
752	Emma E. Wood	Letter from church in Pomfret, Vt.		"	
753	Julia A. Wood	"			
754	Henrietta E. Wood	"			
755	Franklin Wood	Letter from church in Albion, N Y	Mar. 1853		July 1883
756	Almira W. Wood	Letter from church in Alstead, N H	May 1843	Died in Keene	Dec. 1862
757	Samuel Woods	Letter from church in Harrisville, N H	Nov. 1866	Present member	Mar. 1867
758	Harriet G. Woods	"		"	Oct. "
759	Dinsmana Woodward	Profession of faith	Jan. 1833	Died in Swanzey, N H	
760	Asenath Woodward	Letter from church in Grafton, Mass	Nov. 1837	Died in Keene	
761	Mary Wright	Profession of faith	Jan. 1832	"	
762	Albert Wright	"	Jan. 1861	To 2d church, Keene	
763	Julia A. Wright	"			
764	Maria A. Wright	Letter from church in Eastford, Conn	May 1861	Present member	
765	Sarah Wright	Profession of faith	July 1840	Died in Keene	Oct. 1867
766	Charles Wyman	"	May 1843	Present member	
767	Mary A. Wyman	"		"	
768	Henry I. Wyman	"	May 1856	To 2d church, Keene	Oct. 1867
769	Ellen M. Wyman	"		"	
770	Chauncey M. Wyman	"	May 1861	Died in Keene	Sept. 1870
771	J. Louise Wyman	"	Mar. 1864	"	
772	Fanny E. Wyman	"	July 1861	Joined Adventts	May 1868
773	Elsie (Bingham) Wyman	Letter from church in Gilsum, N H	Mar. 1858	Died in Peterboro', N H	Sept. 1875
774	Maria A. (Wilder) Wyman	Profession of faith	Jan. 1848	Died in Keene	Sept. 1858

7

NAMES OF PRESENT RESIDENT MEMBERS.

The numbers of the names in this list correspond to the numbers in the preceding list.

A.

8   Adams, Mary Ann
13 Albee, Holland
14 Albee, Marcia S.
17 Allen, Susan W.
18 Atwood, Hannah W.
19 Ayer, Nancy

71 Bridgman, Sarah H
72 Bridgman. Gertrude H.
75 Briggs, Mary L.
77 Briggs, John K.
78 Briggs, Lydia A.
79 Briggs, Mary C.
93 Buckminster, Harriet I.
94 Buckminster, Charles W.
92 Buckminster, Emily E.
95 Buffum, Addie I.
98 Burgess, Sarah E.
99 Burnap, Harriet
100 Burton, Wellington R.
101 Buss, Mary H.
105 Butterfield, Caroline S.

B.

21 Baker, Amanda H.
22 Baker, Emily F.
23 Bancroft, Ellen E.
29 Barrett, Marla F.
33 Batchelder, John A.
34 Batchelder, Almina R.
35 Batchelder, Clara L.
37 Beal, Lois W.
38 Beckley, Mary J.
48 Blake, Hannah T.
53 Bodwell, Ada M.
55 Boles, Lauretta M.
56 Bolster, Phebe P.
60 Bradford, Samuel W.
61 Bradford, Sarah G.
70 Bridgman, Charles

C.

106 Calef, David R.
108 Carleton, William P.
110 Chamberlain, Dolly
112 Chapman, Lois
115 Chase, Mary
117 Chase, Hannah
122 Chase, Joseph
123 Chase, Victoria B.
129 Clark, Cornelia F.
130 Clark, Edwin H.
131 Clark, Fanny M.
133 Colony, Sarah R.
134 Colony, Eunice J.
140 Cook, Erastus H.
141 Cook, Mary M.
142 Cook, Minnie
148 Cross, Lucy J.
150 Cummings, Maria H.

D.

161 Darling, Sarah L.
165 Day, James C.
166 Day, Charlotte E.
168 Dean, Laura C.
170 Dickinson, Oren
171 Dickinson, Emily H.
172 Dickinson, Abbott W.
173 Dickinson, Addie E.
176 Dort, Eli

177 Dort, Caroline E.
178 Dort, George G.
179 Dort, Eva J.
180 Dort, Mary E.

E.

189 Elliott, Lucretia M.
191 Ellis, Eugene S.
193 Ellis, John
194 Ellis, Pamelia

F.

204 Fay, Franklin
205 Fay, Jennie
211 Flint, Frances A.
213 Forbush, Sarah H.
214 Foster, Stearns
215 Foster, Mary
218 Foster, Mary G.
219 Foster, Charles M.
221 Foster, Frank E.
222 Foster, Ruth A.

G.

243 Geddes, Loretta M.
244 Gerould, Samuel A.
246 Gerould, Samuel A. Jr.
247 Gerould, Susan F.
255 Gould, Grace A.
256 Gould, Cora J.
262 Green, Silas B.
263 Green, Caroline L.
267 Griffin, Helen M.
270 Griffith, Rosina C.
279 Grimes, Mary D.
274 Grimes, Almira
278 Grimes, Frances E.
280 Grinnell, Marion F.

327 Holbrook, Mary A.
328 Holbrook, Lestina M.
329 Holmes, George
331 Holmes, Mary L.
333 Holt, Joseph S.
334 Holt, Celestia M.
337 Howe, Betsey
340 Howland, Martha H.
341 Howland, Eliza A.
346 Hudson, Rosetta P.
347 Humphrey, John
348 Humphrey, Eunice
349 Humphrey, Marietta
351 Hunnewell, Alma C.
354 Hurd, Julia E.
360 Hyde, Charles W.
361 Hyde, Frances M.

H.

284 Haile, Sebrana S.
290 Ham, Samuel
291 Ham, Diantha W.
298 Hastings, Calvin
299 Hastings, Eliza B.
300 Hastings, Calvin W.
301 Hastings, Fred. E.
304 Hayward, Edward
305 Hayward, Emily
306 Healey, Daniel K.
307 Healey, Emma R.
308 Heaton, Harriet
313 Hills, Sarah D.
315 Hills, Francis H.
314 Hills, Ellen M.
316 Hirsch, Cornelia I.
317 Hitchcock, Rufus C.
318 Hitchcock, Louise St. J.
320 Hodgkins, Ambrose
321 Hodgkins, Lois L. W.
323 Holbrook, George E.
324 Holbrook, Clara A.

I.

363 Irish, Horace N.
364 Irish, Eliza E.
365 Isham, Gardner W.
366 Isham, Sarah J.

J.

373 Jones, Robert C
374 Jones, Mary A. H.
377 Joslin, Lydia S.
378 Joslin, Susan A.
379 Joslin, Sarah R.
380 Joslin. Sarah H.

K.

387 Kenney, Thomas M.
390 Keyes, Elizabeth E.
391 Keyes, Clara I.
393 Kidder, Arba
394 Kidder, Mary E.
397 Kingman, Lucinda R.
398 Kingman, Sarah E.
403 Kingsbury, Albert
404 Kingsbury, Ann E.
408 Kingsbury, Mary H.

L.

414 Lane, Rachel I.
412 Lane, Elisha F.
413 Lane, Harriet P.
417 Leland, Patty
418 Leonard, Martha A.
419 Leverett, Abby B.
420 Leverett, Kate F.

424 Loveland, Henrietta V.
426 Lyman, Rosina W.
427 Lyman, Anna K.
428 Lyman, Lizzie G.
429 Lyman, Elizabeth T.

M.

433 Marsh, Candace
434 Marsh, Walter E.
435 Marshall, Ella
438 Maynard, Rhoda
439 McAllister, Jennie M.
443 McLane, Mary L. W.
446 Metcalf, Edwin G.
447 Metcalf, Martha S.
448 Metcalf, William
449 Metcalf, Amanda
450 Metcalf, Alvah E.
451 Metcalf, Harriet M.
452 Metcalf. Thankful
455 Metcalf, Sarah E.
457 Morrison, Betsey
458 Morrison, Julia A.
459 Morrison, Sarah

N.

465 Newell, Rebecca
476 Nims, Ainsworth M.
477 Nims, George H.
478 Nims, Ruth A.
479 Nims, Francis O.
480 Nims, Ella L.
481 Noble. Lewis C.

O.

488 Olcott, Mary

P.

495 Page, Silas
497 Page, Lydia H.
507 Parker, Mary K.
510 Patterson, Harvey F.
511 Patterson, Helen M.
516 Phelps, Lois W.
520 Phillips, Harvey
521 Phillips, Elvira
525 Pierce, Sophia C.
527 Pond, Sophronia E.
528 Poole, Elvira P.
529 Porter, Ellen E.
532 Porter, Alice G.
534 Pray, Charlotte M.
539 Proctor, Jane E.

R.

551 Ranney, Deborah D. G.
553 Reed, Joel
554 Reed, Helen M.
556 Rest, Susan
557 Rhodes, Melinda F.
559 Richardson, Elvira
562 Richardson, Cyrus
563 Richardson, Annie D.
564 Richards, Clara H.
565 Ripley, Barrett
566 Ripley, Mary C.
567 Ripley, Franklin
568 Ripley, Mary R.
569 Ripley, Harriet B.
570 Ripley, Martha B.

573 Robinson, Clara E.
577 Rugg, Frank A.
582 Russell, Delia I. T.

S.

583 Sargent, Flora E.
585 Saunders, Mary
591 Sears, Andrew C.
592 Sears, Julia A.
594 Sheldon, Frances A.
595 Shelley, Roana
597 Sherman, Ida M.
602 Skinner, Betsey
603 Skinner, Azro B.
604 Skinner, Sophie C.
617 Spalter, Martha A. H.
618 Spalter, Addie C.
619 Spalter, Mary G.
620 Spalter, Wilton H.
621 Spalter, Emma A.
627 Spaulding, Lisette W.
628 Spear, Lois S.
629 Stone, Solon W.
631 Stone, Gertrude E.
632 Stone, Charles W.
636 Sturtevant, Lindamira
637 Sturtevant, Isabella L.
638 Sturtevant, Ellen M.
641 Symonds, Caroline R.

T.

655 Thompson, Sally
656 Thompson, Emma J.
658 Tilden, Cynthia L.
659 Tilden, Laura B.
660 Tilden, Kate L.
674 Towne, Harriet W.
677 Tuttle, Leonard J.
678 Tuttle, Susan M.

W.

683 Wellington, Leonard
684 Wellington, Hattie L.
685 Wellman, Jerry P.
700 White, Shubael
701 White, Nancy L.
703 White, Frederic A.
708 Whitney, Charles H.
709 Whitney, Lucy C.
710 Whitney, Charles R.
719 Wilder, Susan M.
720 Wilkinson, Solon S.
721 Wilkinson, Chestina B.
722 Wilkinson, Edward H.
725 Willard, William
726 Willard, Lucretia M.

727 Willard, Sally H.
729 Willard, Aurelia T.
730 Willard, Lucy R.
731 Willard, Katie J.
733 Willson, Jehiel
734 Willson, Lucy C.
735 Willson, Mary E.
736 Willson, Helen E.
737 Wilson, Eliza
740 Wilson, William O.
741 Wilson, Harriet M.
742 Wilson, Abbie M.
750 Wood, Sarah L.
752 Wood, Emma E.
753 Wood, Julia A.
755 Wood, Franklin
754 Wood, Henrietta E.
757 Woods, Samuel
758 Woods, Harriet G.
764 Wright, Maria A.
766 Wyman, Charles
767 Wyman, Mary A.
771 Wyman, J Louisa

Resident members, - - - - - - -	294
Non-resident members, - - - - - -	36
Total, - - - - - - - -	330